The Tragedy of Macbeth

Side-by-Side Edition

WILLIAM SHAKESPEARE

Translated into Modern English by
Scott Cowie

The characters and events portrayed in this book are fictitious. Any similarity to real persons, living or dead, is coincidental and not intended by the author.

Cover design by: Scott Cowie
Cover image: PublicDomainPictures/Pixabay

ISBN: 9798663842372

THE TRAGEDY OF MACBETH

INTRODUCTION

Shakespeare is widely regarded as the greatest ever writer in the English language. However, since his plays were written over four hundred years ago, the language he uses can be difficult for the modern reader to decipher. Whilst a large part of his plays' appeal relates to his poetical use of language, perhaps even more of it derives from the fact that he wrote such rollicking good tales.

Each of Shakespeare's plays has all the elements that modern audiences find seductive in the latest Netflix, or whatever your streaming service of choice, series. They all have fascinating characters - heroes to love, villains to hate (but also often to sympathise with), love interests and comic buffoons – fast-moving and suspenseful plots, and references to current events. And all this is packaged together in a way that audiences can intimately relate to their own lives.

But, yes, despite these characteristics, it must be admitted that Shakespearean language can be very dense, complex and difficult to understand, especially for the uninitiated and the inexperienced. That's why in this side by side edition of Macbeth, Shakespeare's wonderful play has been translated into modern English next to Shakespeare's original text, so that everyone can engage with this remarkable story and easily comprehend its plot, character development and imagery.

In this side by side translation, not only are words updated to their more modern counterparts, I have also simplified the syntax, extended the language to include full details of the references to famous contemporaries of Shakespeare, and the cultural and social practices that may have been readily understood in his day, but are utterly incomprehensible to most modern readers. This has, I hope, alleviated the need for distracting and ugly in-text notes and glossaries.

I have also been careful to maintain the integrity of Shakespeare's imagery, such as his metaphors, that add so much to our understanding of the characters, and the plot. Also, where Shakespeare has used rhyme, I have tended to use rhyme as well, as, especially with regards to the witches, this is a core component of their portrayal. Rhyme also tends to be employed to conclude scenes. I have likewise tried to ensure that the fast-paced engaging nature of the play is maintained, and this has sometimes required shifting the emphasis of the language used from Shakespeare's, in order to maintain the intent, if not the specifics, of the language used.

Macbeth is a fantastic story, and if the characters do not seem engaging and life-like, if you are not absolutely hooked, and on tenterhooks dying to know what happens to them, then I have clearly failed with my translation. I have also maintained the format as drama, as trying to novelise the story would inevitably draw it too far from the original, and make it less a referable translation, than a standalone reworking. However, I have taken the liberty of extending the scene directions so that they provide more comprehensive descriptions of the location and scenery, which perhaps provide a slight narrative tone.

Whether you are reading this translation because it is an assigned text for your English class at school, or you are a non-native English speaker nervous about engaging with a text written in what may seem to be another language entirely from modern English, or if you are just a general reader, who has, intimidated, avoided Shakespeare so far, but realised that you can no longer, or perhaps you have booked tickets to the latest production at the theatre for your partner and want to impress them by understanding the story before you go, then this translation is for you.

I hope that you'll find this modern translation not only interesting as a story in itself, but also that it encourages you, and gives you the confidence, to attempt to engage with Shakespeare in his original language. For no matter how proud I may be of this translation, it can never compare in any way to the brilliance of the original.

Whilst it may be tempting for me to give you a summary of the background to Macbeth's story, the political and social situation in eleventh-century Scotland, or equally the background to Shakespeare's life, and the political and social situation in late sixteenth-century England, I believe this may be more of a hindrance than a benefit. No, it is for the better, I believe, for you to dive right in. There is no need to be intimidated by the story or the language. This will be as simple to read and understand as any contemporary text you may come across.

If, once you've read it, it makes you want to understand more about the real story of Macbeth, or details of Shakespeare's own life, then I have achieved my aim. There are a number of such resources available freely online, and I highly recommend that you avail yourself of them in the future.

But, without further ado, I welcome you to the tragedy of Macbeth

CHARACTERS OF THE PLAY

KING DUNCAN, *The King of Scotland.*
MALCOLM, *Duncan's Son.*
DONALBAIN, *Duncan's Son.*
MACBETH, *Lord of Glamis, then Lord of Cawdor, then King of Scotland.*
LADY MACBETH, *Macbeth's wife.*
BANQUO, *General of the King's Army.*
MACDUFF, *Scottish Lord.*
LADY MACDUFF, *Macduff's wife.*
LENNOX, *Scottish Lord.*
ROSS, *Scottish Lord.*
MENTEITH, *Scottish Lord.*
ANGUS, *Scottish Lord.*
CAITHNESS, *Scottish Lord.*
FLEANCE, *Banquo's Son.*
SIWARD, *Earl of Northumberland, English General.*
YOUNG SIWARD, *Earl of Northumberland's Son.*
SEYTON, *Macbeth's Servant.*
HECATE, *Queen of the Witches,*
Macduff's Son.
An English Doctor.
A Scottish Doctor.
A Captain.
A Porter.
An Old Man.
Lady Macbeth's Maid.
Six Witches.
Various Lords, Soldiers, Murderers, Attendants & Messengers.
Banquo's Ghost and several other Apparitions

ACT ONE

SCENE ONE

We are in a barren rural landscape in eleventh-century Scotland. There is thunder and lightning and generally wild weather. It is dark and stormy. And there are three Witches.

MODERN TRANSLATION:

(1-2) **FIRST WITCH.**
When will we three all meet again,
In thunder, lightning or in rain?

(3-4) **SECOND WITCH.**
When this fiasco is all done,
And the battle's been lost or won.

(5) **THIRD WITCH.**
So, that's before the setting sun.

(6) **FIRST WITCH.**
Where's the place?

(6) **SECOND WITCH.**
In the scrubland.

ORIGINAL LANGUAGE:

(1-2) FIRST WITCH.
When shall we three meet again?
In thunder, lightning, or in rain?

(3-4) SECOND WITCH.
When the hurlyburly's done,
When the battle's lost and won.

(5) THIRD WITCH.
That will be ere the set of sun.

(6) FIRST WITCH.
Where the place?

(6) SECOND WITCH.
Upon the heath.

(7) **THIRD WITCH.**
That's where we'll meet Macbeth.

(7) THIRD WITCH.
There to meet with Macbeth.

(8) **FIRST WITCH.**
I'm coming, Grimalkin, my pussy cat.

(8) FIRST WITCH.
I come, Graymalkin!

(9) **SECOND WITCH.**
And I hear my pet toad, Paddock, calling me.

(9) SECOND WITCH.
Paddock calls.

(9) **THIRD WITCH.**
Come on, let's go.

(9) THIRD WITCH.
Anon

(10-11) **ALL.**
Fair is foul, and foul is fair,
We fly through fog and filthy air.

(10-11) ALL.
Fair is foul, and foul is fair:
Hover through the fog and filthy air.

The Witches vanish into the dark and murky sky.

ACT ONE

SCENE TWO

At an army barracks near Forres, in Scotland, where the King's army is fighting Irish, Norwegian and treacherous Scottish rebels. King Duncan arrives on the scene, to the sound of trumpets, with Malcolm, Donalbain, Lennox, and various attendants. They meet a bleeding captain come straight from the battlefront.

MODERN TRANSLATION:

ORIGINAL LANGUAGE:

(1-3) **KING DUNCAN.**
Who's that bleeding man? Perhaps a soldier who can tell us the latest news from the front?

(1-3) **DUNCAN.**
What bloody man is that? He can report,
As seemeth by his plight, of the revolt
The newest state.

(3-7) **MALCOLM.**
This, your majesty, is the captain who like a tough and courageous soldier fought bravely to free me from my captivity.

Welcome, my brave friend. Please proceed to tell the King the latest news of the war.

(3-7) **MALCOLM.**
This is the sergeant
Who, like a good and hardy soldier, fought
'Gainst my captivity.—Hail, brave friend!
Say to the King the knowledge of the broil
As thou didst leave it.

(7-23) **A CAPTAIN.**

Well, things were a bit tricky at the start. It was like two exhausted swimmers grabbing at each other, each one forcing the other down, and yet neither saving himself. And that rebel Macdonald, well he was a ruthless rebel. He's as evil as any of his chums that have joined him from Ireland. Yes, he has many soldiers and militiamen with him. And it did look like lady luck was on Macdonald's side, but, sir, lady luck is unfaithful, isn't she?

It did turn out that none of the enemy were a match for our brave Macbeth. Oh, and brave he was! He didn't worry about luck. Yes, he was dreadfully courageous with his fiery sword. He carved his way through that field till he faced his foe.

And he didn't bother to shake his hand or say goodbye. He simply sliced him from his head to his toe and stuck his decapitated head on the end of his sword.

(7-23) ***SOLDIER.***
Doubtful it stood;
As two spent swimmers that do cling together
And choke their art. The merciless Macdonwald
(Worthy to be a rebel, for to that
The multiplying villainies of nature
Do swarm upon him) from the Western Isles
Of kerns and gallowglasses is supplied;
And Fortune, on his damned quarrel smiling,
Show'd like a rebel's whore. But all's too weak;
For brave Macbeth (well he deserves that name),
Disdaining Fortune, with his brandish'd steel,
Which smok'd with bloody execution,
Like Valour's minion, carv'd out his passage,
Till he fac'd the slave;
Which ne'er shook hands, nor bade farewell to him,
Till he unseam'd him from the nave to the chops,
And fix'd his head upon our battlements.

(24) **KING DUNCAN.**
Oh, you brave boy, my noble Macbeth.

(24) ***DUNCAN.***
O valiant cousin! worthy gentleman!

(25-33) **A CAPTAIN.**
But just as the start of spring can often bring us thunder and stormy seas, so too did this bright day bring us a grey dawn, your majesty. Yes, hear this, no sooner had our brave Macbeth dished out justice and made the enemy flee, then the Norwegian king, seeing his chance, attacked us with his large army. You know those Norwegians, with their ostentatious armour and all.

(25-33) ***SOLDIER.***
As whence the sun 'gins his reflection
Shipwracking storms and direful thunders break,
So from that spring, whence comfort seem'd to come
Discomfort swells. Mark, King of Scotland, mark:
No sooner justice had, with valour arm'd,
Compell'd these skipping kerns to trust their heels,
But the Norweyan lord, surveying vantage,
With furbish'd arms and new supplies of men,
Began a fresh assault.

(34) **KING DUNCAN.**
Did this not cause great concern to our captains, Macbeth and Banquo?

(34) ***DUNCAN.***
Dismay'd not this
Our captains, Macbeth and Banquo?

(35-42) **A CAPTAIN.**
It concerned them about as much as a sparrow concerns an eagle, sir, or a rabbit a lion!

To tell you the truth, they were a bit like a cannon with double the gunpowder. They gave our foe double the woe! It was as if they wanted a battlefield that could be compared to Golgotha, where, as you know, Jesus, our saviour was crucified. You wouldn't believe it, but…

Though with my wounds and this loss of blood and all, I'm feeling a little faint, sir.

(35-42) ***SOLDIER.***
Yes;
As sparrows eagles, or the hare the lion.
If I say sooth, I must report they were

As cannons overcharg'd with double cracks;
So they
Doubly redoubled strokes upon the foe:
Except they meant to bathe in reeking wounds,
Or memorize another Golgotha,
I cannot tell—
But I am faint, my gashes cry for help.

(43-45) **KING DUNCAN.**
Your wounds are as worthy as the news you've told us.

To his attendants.
Please, go fetch a doctor to see to him.

The captain departs with King Duncan's attendants. Ross and Angus arrive.

Who's that coming?

(43-45) ***DUNCAN.***
So well thy words become thee as thy wounds:
They smack of honour both.—Go, get him surgeons.

Exit Captain, attended.
Enter Ross and Angus.

Who comes here?

(45) **MALCOLM.**
It is the noble Lord of Ross.

(45) ***MALCOLM.***
The worthy Thane of Ross.

(46-47) **LENNOX.**
He walks like a man on a mission. Look at his eyes. I expect he has something unexpected to tell us.

(46-47) ***LENNOX.***
What a haste looks through his eyes! So should he look
That seems to speak things strange.

(47) **ROSS.**
God save the King!

(47) ***ROSS.***
God save the King!

(48) **KING DUNCAN.**
Where have you come from Lord Ross?

(48) ***DUNCAN.***

Whence cam'st thou, worthy thane?

(48-58) **ROSS.**
From Fife, my King, where the Norwegian Flag was fluttering, fanning our citizens in fear. The King of Norway himself took to battle, with his large army, and aided by that traitor, the Lord of Cawdor. Oh, it did look like they had our number.

But then, worthy Macbeth in armour arrived on the scene. And he dealt that invader swift vengeance. Sword vs sword. Arm vs arm. Macbeth was brave. And, as you can imagine, victory was soon ours.

(48-58) ***ROSS.***
From Fife, great King,
Where the Norweyan banners flout the sky
And fan our people cold.
Norway himself, with terrible numbers,
Assisted by that most disloyal traitor,
The Thane of Cawdor, began a dismal conflict;
Till that Bellona's bridegroom, lapp'd in proof,
Confronted him with self-comparisons,
Point against point, rebellious arm 'gainst arm,
Curbing his lavish spirit: and, to conclude,
The victory fell on us.

(58) **KING DUNCAN.**
What marvellous news!

(58) ***DUNCAN.***
Great happiness!

(58-62) **ROSS.**
After that, the Norwegian King, Sweno, was simply begging us for a truce. But we wouldn't even allow him to bury his own men, till he retreated and paid us ten thousand dollars' in ransom.

(58-62) ***ROSS.***
That now
Sweno, the Norways' king, craves composition;
Nor would we deign him burial of his men
Till he disbursed at Saint Colme's Inch
Ten thousand dollars to our general use.

(63-65) **KING DUNCAN.**
Well that Lord of Cawdor won't bother us

again. Off with his head and pass his title onto the new Lord of Cawdor: the worthy Macbeth!

(63-65) ***DUNCAN.***
No more that Thane of Cawdor shall deceive
Our bosom interest. Go pronounce his present death,
And with his former title greet Macbeth.

(66) **ROSS.**
Your highness, I'll see that it is done.

(66) ***ROSS.***
I'll see it done.

(67) **KING DUNCAN.**
What Cawdor has lost, brave Macbeth has won.

(67) ***DUNCAN.***
What he hath lost, noble Macbeth hath won.

They each return to their allotted places within the barracks.

ACT ONE

SCENE THREE

There is thunder and lightning and generally wild weather. We are in a barren field. It is dark. And there are the three Witches again.

MODERN TRANSLATION:

ORIGINAL LANGUAGE:

(1) **FIRST WITCH.**
Where have you been, sister?

(1) FIRST WITCH.
Where hast thou been, sister?

(2) **SECOND WITCH.**
Killing pigs.

(2) SECOND WITCH.
Killing swine.

(2) **THIRD WITCH.**
What about you, sister?

(2) THIRD WITCH.
Sister, where thou?

(3-9) **FIRST WITCH.**
A sailor's wife was eating peanuts. Munch, munch, munch. "Give me some," said I. But "go away witch," said that fat-arsed cow. Well, I know her husband's sailing to Aleppo, the captain of a ship called the Tiger.

In a sieve away I'll sail,
Like a rat without a tail,
And do him some harm without fail.

(3-9) FIRST WITCH.
A sailor's wife had chestnuts in her lap,
And munch'd, and munch'd, and munch'd. "Give me," quoth I.

"Aroint thee, witch!" the rump-fed ronyon cries.
Her husband's to Aleppo gone, master o' th' Tiger:_
But in a sieve I'll thither sail,
And, like a rat without a tail,
I'll do, I'll do, and I'll do.

(10) **SECOND WITCH.**
I'll give you my wind.

(10) SECOND WITCH.
I'll give thee a wind.

(11) **FIRST WITCH.**
You are too kind.

(11) FIRST WITCH.
Th'art kind.

(12) **THIRD WITCH.**
Me too, I'll give you mine.

(12) THIRD WITCH.
And I another.

(13-24) **FIRST WITCH.**
Well, all the other winds are mine.
And the ports they blow through and pass.
I know all the routes of the compass.
I'll drain that sailor dry as hay,
Never to sleep more, night nor day.
His eyelids open, never pursed,
He'll live on like a man who's cursed.
For sad lonely weeks, nine times nine
He'll cry, starve and for some hope pine.
Though I cannot make his ship sink,
He'll be living right on the brink.
Look at what I have.

(13-24) FIRST WITCH.
I myself have all the other,
And the very ports they blow,
All the quarters that they know
I' the shipman's card.
I will drain him dry as hay:
Sleep shall neither night nor day
Hang upon his pent-house lid;
He shall live a man forbid.
Weary sev'n-nights nine times nine,
Shall he dwindle, peak, and pine:
Though his bark cannot be lost,
Yet it shall be tempest-tost.
Look what I have.

(25) **SECOND WITCH.**
Show me, show me.

(25) ***SECOND WITCH.***
Show me, show me.

(26-27) **FIRST WITCH.**
See, here I have a captain's thumb,
Whom I shipwrecked when he did come.

A drum is heard.

(26-27) ***FIRST WITCH.***
Here I have a pilot's thumb,
Wrack'd as homeward he did come.

Drum within.

(28-29) **THIRD WITCH.**
A drum, a drum,
Macbeth does come.

(28-29) ***THIRD WITCH.***
A drum, a drum!
Macbeth doth come.

(30-35) **ALL THE WITCHES.** *Dancing in a circle.*
The fateful sisters, hand in hand,
Travellers of the sea and land.
We all do go about, about
It's three for you, and three for mine
And three again to make up nine.
Quiet! Our spell is done.

Macbeth and Banquo enter riding their horses.

(30-35) ***ALL.***
The Weird Sisters, hand in hand,
Posters of the sea and land,
Thus do go about, about:
Thrice to thine, and thrice to mine,
And thrice again, to make up nine.
Peace!—the charm's wound up.

Enter Macbeth and Banquo.

(36) **MACBETH.** *To Banquo.*
I've never experienced a day that's been so fair in its successes, and yet so foul in its weather.

(36) ***MACBETH.***

So foul and fair a day I have not seen.

(37-44) **BANQUO.** *To Macbeth.*
How far is it to the town of Forres?

He notices the Witches.
What is this I see? So old, so withered and so wildly dressed. They look like aliens, yet they are here on earth.

They look foreign to me. Though they do seem to understand me, judging by the way they lay their shrivelled-up fingers to their thin, dry lips. They look like women, although their beards do suggest otherwise.

(37-44) BANQUO.
How far is't call'd to Forres?—What are these,
So wither'd, and so wild in their attire,
That look not like the inhabitants o' th' earth,
And yet are on't?—Live you? or are you aught
That man may question? You seem to understand me,
By each at once her choppy finger laying
Upon her skinny lips. You should be women,
And yet your beards forbid me to interpret
That you are so.

(45) **MACBETH.** *To the Witches.*
Speak, if you can. What are you?

(45) MACBETH.
Speak, if you can;—what are you?

(46) **FIRST WITCH.**
All hail Macbeth! Hail to you the Lord of Gamis!

(46) FIRST WITCH.
All hail, Macbeth! hail to thee, Thane of Glamis!

(47) **SECOND WITCH.**
All hail Macbeth! Hail to you the Lord of Cawdor!

(47) SECOND WITCH.
All hail, Macbeth! hail to thee, Thane of Cawdor!

(45) **THIRD WITCH.**
All hail Macbeth! That will be king!

(45) THIRD WITCH.
All hail, Macbeth! that shalt be king hereafter!

(49-59) **BANQUO.** *To Macbeth.*

Oh, come on Macbeth, why do you look so worried when they tell you such wondrous news.

To the Witches.
In the name of God, are you spirits real, or are you as unreal as you appear? You greet my friend here with great titles, and forecast a royal role for him. And while he does seem entranced by this news, you don't, on the other hand, speak to me at all. If you can see into the future and predict our fortunes, then tell me mine too. I don't care if you tell me of good or of ill.

(49-59) ***BANQUO.***
Good sir, why do you start and seem to fear
Things that do sound so fair?—I' th' name of truth,
Are ye fantastical, or that indeed
Which outwardly ye show? My noble partner
You greet with present grace and great prediction
Of noble having and of royal hope,
That he seems rapt withal. To me you speak not.
If you can look into the seeds of time,
And say which grain will grow, and which will not,
Speak then to me, who neither beg nor fear
Your favours nor your hate

(60) **FIRST WITCH.**
Hail!

(60) ***FIRST WITCH.***
Hail!

(61) **SECOND WITCH.**
Hail!

(61) ***SECOND WITCH.***
Hail!

(62) **THIRD WITCH.**
Hail!

(62) ***THIRD WITCH.***
Hail!

(63) **FIRST WITCH.**
Less than Macbeth, yet much greater.

(63) ***FIRST WITCH.***
Lesser than Macbeth, and greater.

(64) **SECOND WITCH.**
Not as happy, but much happier.

(64) ***SECOND WITCH.***

Not so happy, yet much happier.

(65-66) **THIRD WITCH.**
You'll father kings, but not be one yourself.
So all hail! Banquo and Macbeth!

(65-66) THIRD WITCH.
Thou shalt get kings, though thou be none:
So all hail, Macbeth and Banquo!

(67) **FIRST WITCH.**
Macbeth and Banquo! All hail!

(67) FIRST WITCH.
Banquo and Macbeth, all hail!

(68-76) **MACBETH.**
Wait, you mysterious prophets. Please explain to me a little more. I know I am Lord of Glamis due to my father's death. But why Lord of Cawdor? The Lord of Cawdor is still alive.

And what a wealthy man he is…

But to be king, well that beggars belief! Why do you tell me these things? And where did you get this knowledge? And why, in this horrid field, do you bother us with your potty predictions.

Speak now witches!

The Witches vanish into the air.

(68-76) MACBETH.
Stay, you imperfect speakers, tell me more.
By Sinel's death I know I am Thane of Glamis;
But how of Cawdor? The Thane of Cawdor lives,
A prosperous gentleman; and to be king
Stands not within the prospect of belief,
No more than to be Cawdor. Say from whence
You owe this strange intelligence? or why
Upon this blasted heath you stop our way
With such prophetic greeting?—Speak, I charge you.

Witches vanish.

(77-78) **BANQUO.**
The earth has bubbles, just like water does. And bubbles were they. Who could possibly know where they've gone?

(77-78) BANQUO.

The earth hath bubbles, as the water has,
And these are of them. Whither are they vanish'd?

(79-80) **MACBETH.**
Into the air, and what had just then seemed real, has melted, like our breath, into the wind. I wish they'd stayed to tell us more.

(79-80) MACBETH.
Into the air; and what seem'd corporal,
Melted as breath into the wind.
Would they had stay'd!

(81-83) **BANQUO.**
Were they really here, or did we just imagine them? Or have we been given some kind of drug that has robbed us of our senses?

(81-83) BANQUO.
Were such things here as we do speak about?
Or have we eaten on the insane root
That takes the reason prisoner?

(84) **MACBETH.**
Your children will be Kings.

(84) MACBETH.
Your children shall be kings.

(84) **BANQUO.**
You will be King.

(84) BANQUO.
You shall be king

(85) **MACBETH.**
And Lord of Cawdor too. Is that not what they said?

(85) MACBETH.
And Thane of Cawdor too; went it not so?

(86) **BANQUO.**
That is exactly what they said.

Who's this?

Ross and Angus enter on their horses.

(86) BANQUO.
To the selfsame tune and words. Who's here?

Enter Ross and Angus.

(87-98) **ROSS.**
The King has heard the happy news, Macbeth. The news of your triumphs has spread far and

wide. And when he considers your exploits, your feats in the face of those rebels, well, he does not know whether to speak of how unbelievable it all is, or instead of how much he appreciates it all, so he just remains mute in his overwhelming shock, and says absolutely nothing at all.

And then he hears of your triumphs against the Norwegians. We're told that you had no fear of death, and that it was a quick and brutal death that you dealt to the enemy. As thick as hail where the announcements he received of your brave deeds. And all of these plainly certified your foremost role in Scotland's defence. The tributes given, well, they poured down upon the King as if he were drowning in a flood of your praises.

(87-98) **ROSS.**
The King hath happily receiv'd, Macbeth,
The news of thy success, and when he reads
Thy personal venture in the rebels' fight,
His wonders and his praises do contend
Which should be thine or his: silenc'd with that,
In viewing o'er the rest o' th' selfsame day,
He finds thee in the stout Norweyan ranks,
Nothing afeard of what thyself didst make,
Strange images of death. As thick as tale
Came post with post; and everyone did bear
Thy praises in his kingdom's great defence,
And pour'd them down before him.

(98-101) **ANGUS.**
Macbeth, we have been sent by the King to thank you. Not to deliver you a reward, but to deliver you to him.

(98-101) **ANGUS.**
We are sent
To give thee from our royal master thanks;
Only to herald thee into his sight,
Not pay thee.

(102-105) **ROSS.**
We've also been sent to tell you of a great honour bestowed on you. You are the new Lord of Cawdor. We therefore hail you as this, our worthy Lord of Cawdor!

(102-105) ***ROSS.***
And, for an earnest of a greater honour,
He bade me, from him, call thee Thane of Cawdor:
In which addition, hail, most worthy thane,
For it is thine.

(105) **BANQUO.** *To Macbeth.*
What, did those witches speak the truth?

(105) ***BANQUO.***
What, can the devil speak true?

(106-107) **MACBETH.**
The Lord of Cawdor still lives. Why dress me in borrowed robes?

(106-107) ***MACBETH.***
The Thane of Cawdor lives: why do you dress me
In borrow'd robes?

(107-114) **ANGUS.**
While he may technically still be alive, sir, he has been sentenced to death, and deservedly so. Whether he aligned himself with the Norwegians, or secretly supported the rebels with support and intelligence, or did both, he undoubtedly conspired to bring about Scotland's ruin. Though it's not for me to say, his treasons have been proven, he's confessed, and now he's been overthrown.

(107-114) ***ANGUS.***
Who was the Thane lives yet,
But under heavy judgement bears that life
Which he deserves to lose. Whether he was combin'd
With those of Norway, or did line the rebel
With hidden help and vantage, or that with both
He labour'd in his country's wrack, I know not;
But treasons capital, confess'd and prov'd,
Have overthrown him.

(114-118) **MACBETH.** *To himself.*
Lord of Glamis and Cawdor? The best is yet to come.

To Ross and Angus.
Thank you for this news, men.

To Banquo.

Do you not now believe that your children will be kings? Those who promised me the lordship of Cawdor, promised that to you.

(114-118) ***MACBETH.***
Aside:
Glamis, and Thane of Cawdor:
The greatest is behind.

To Ross and Angus:
Thanks for your pains.

To Banquo:
Do you not hope your children shall be kings,
When those that gave the Thane of Cawdor to me
Promis'd no less to them?

(118-125) **BANQUO.**
And if we accept all their prophecies, that means you will soon be King Macbeth, as well.

But it is strange though. Sometimes, to bring us to our downfall, our rivals will flatter our vanities with the words we crave the most. But this is often ultimately done solely to put us on a path to our destruction.

To Ross and Angus.
May I please have a word alone with you both?

(118-125) ***BANQUO.***
That, trusted home,
Might yet enkindle you unto the crown,
Besides the Thane of Cawdor. But 'tis strange:
And oftentimes to win us to our harm,
The instruments of darkness tell us truths;
Win us with honest trifles, to betray's
In deepest consequence.—
Cousins, a word, I pray you.

(126-141) **MACBETH.** *To himself.*
Two truths have been told. But these are nothing but the opening credits before I play the lead role.

To Ross and Angus.
I thank you, gentleman.

To himself.

Yet the witches' mystic predictions seem neither entirely good nor bad. If bad, well, then why has this honour, which they had so deftly prophesied, come directly to me. I am now Lord of Cawdor. But, on the other hand, if it is good, then why am I dogged by thoughts which are making my hairs stand on end, and make my heart beat unnaturally fast.

Yes, my fears at present must only be imaginary. The contemplation, my contemplation, yes, my contemplation, of the King's murder is still nothing but a trivial fantasy.

And yet I can still sense that the contemplation, my contemplation, of it is now beginning to pull apart my mind. But do I even have the capability to act upon this thought?

No, take hold of yourself, Macbeth, nothing is surely quite as it seems.

(126-141) ***MACBETH.***
Aside.
Two truths are told,
As happy prologues to the swelling act
Of the imperial theme.

—I thank you, gentlemen.—

Aside.
This supernatural soliciting
Cannot be ill; cannot be good. If ill,
Why hath it given me earnest of success,
Commencing in a truth? I am Thane of Cawdor:
If good, why do I yield to that suggestion
Whose horrid image doth unfix my hair,
And make my seated heart knock at my ribs,
Against the use of nature? Present fears
Are less than horrible imaginings.
My thought, whose murder yet is but fantastical,
Shakes so my single state of man
That function is smother'd in surmise,
And nothing is but what is not.

(141) **BANQUO.** *To Ross and Angus.*
Look at how excited Macbeth is.

(141) ***BANQUO.***
Look, how our partner's rapt.

(142-143) **MACBETH.** *To himself.*
If I'm prophesied to become king, well, then that then must certainly come to pass whether or not I act out on any impulses that may or may not be stirring within me.

(142-143) ***MACBETH.***
Aside:
If chance will have me king, why, chance may crown me
Without my stir.

(143-145) **BANQUO.** *To Ross and Angus.*
I think these new titles are fitting him like my new shoes fit me. Giving him metaphorical blisters, I mean. But the leather will soon soften as he walks in them more.

(143-145) ***BANQUO.***
New honours come upon him,
Like our strange garments, cleave not to their mould
But with the aid of use.

(145-146) **MACBETH.** *To himself.*
But come what may, what will be will be.

(145-146) ***MACBETH.***
Aside:
Come what come may,
Time and the hour runs through the roughest day.

(147) **BANQUO.**
Brave Macbeth, we are happy to pause whilst you gather your thoughts.

(147) ***BANQUO.***
Worthy Macbeth, we stay upon your leisure.

(148-154) **MACBETH.**
I do beg your pardon. My poor brain is just a little agitated. I have a few minor matters on my mind.

To Ross and Angus.
Gentleman. I thank you for coming. I will never neglect to remember your efforts.

Well, I guess it's time for me to go and meet the King!

To Banquo alone.

We can have a little think about what's we've witnessed, and when we've had the time to reflect on it a bit more, we can speak some more in private.

(148-154) ***MACBETH.***
Give me your favour. My dull brain was wrought
With things forgotten. Kind gentlemen, your pains
Are register'd where every day I turn
The leaf to read them.—Let us toward the King.—
Think upon what hath chanc'd; and at more time,
The interim having weigh'd it, let us speak
Our free hearts each to other.

(155) **BANQUO.**
I look forward to it, sir.

(155) ***BANQUO.***
Very gladly.

(156) **MACBETH.** *To Banquo.*
Till then, my friend.

Banquo, on his horse, exits alone.

To Ross and Angus.
Come on, I want to see the King!

(156) ***MACBETH.***
Till then, enough.—Come, friends.

Macbeth exits on his horse, alongside Ross and Angus.

ACT ONE

SCENE FOUR

We are in a room in King Duncan's palace, in Forres. King Duncan, Lennox, Malcolm, Donalbain and attendants enter ceremoniously.

MODERN TRANSLATION:

ORIGINAL LANGUAGE:

(1-2) **KING DUNCAN.**
Has the Lord of Cawdor been executed yet? Have his executioners returned?

(1-2) KING DUNCAN.
Is execution done on Cawdor? Are not
Those in commission yet return'd?

(2-11) **MALCOLM.**
Your majesty, they have yet to return. But I have spoken with someone who says they saw Cawdor die. Apparently, he also confessed to his treasons and begged for your majesty's pardon. Supposedly he acted as though he was very remorseful.

I believe it's said that he never did anything so well in his life, as he did do his death. He died as one who had already rehearsed it many times, though, as it was not unexpected, I am not surprised.

In the end though, it's true that he has thrown away his life, the thing that must've been dearest to him in the whole world. But it has been thrown away through his treachery as though it were nothing but a disposable triviality.

(2-11) MALCOLM.

My liege,
They are not yet come back. But I have spoke
With one that saw him die, who did report,
That very frankly he confess'd his treasons,
Implor'd your Highness' pardon, and set forth
A deep repentance. Nothing in his life
Became him like the leaving it; he died
As one that had been studied in his death,
To throw away the dearest thing he ow'd
As 'twere a careless trifle.

(11-21) **KING DUNCAN.**
There is obviously no way to tell what a person is thinking by looking at their face. He was a man I trusted absolutely.

Macbeth, Banquo, Ross and Angus enter the room.

Macbeth, my favourite cousin, there is no way that I can repay the debts I owe to you. You are so far ahead of me that even if my thanks were carried upwards on an eagle's wing, they still could not reach your heights of glory.

Yes, if you hadn't done so much, so well, then, well maybe then, I may have been able to reward you according to your true value. But, as it is, all I can say is: 'your worth is more than I can pay'.

(11-21) ***KING DUNCAN.***
There's no art
To find the mind's construction in the face:
He was a gentleman on whom I built
An absolute trust.

Enter Macbeth, Banquo, Ross and Angus.

O worthiest cousin!
The sin of my ingratitude even now
Was heavy on me. Thou art so far before,
That swiftest wing of recompense is slow
To overtake thee. Would thou hadst less deserv'd;
That the proportion both of thanks and payment
Might have been mine! only I have left to say,
More is thy due than more than all can pay.

(22-27) **MACBETH.**
The service and the loyalty that I owe you, your majesty, puts me more in debt to you than I could ever repay. Your true role is only to gladly receive our duties, and all our duty is for you and your throne.

Moreover, the state as a whole does all that it does in its undeserving thanks to you, and to safeguard both your love and your honour.

(22-27) ***MACBETH.***
The service and the loyalty I owe,
In doing it, pays itself. Your Highness' part
Is to receive our duties: and our duties
Are to your throne and state, children and servants;
Which do but what they should, by doing everything
Safe toward your love and honour.

(27-32) **KING DUNCAN.** *To Macbeth.*
Welcome home. You are yet but a sapling, but I will nurture you so that you grow into a great oak.

King Duncan embraces Macbeth.

Noble Banquo, you no less deserve my praise, and you too must be held in the same esteem as Macbeth. So, let me embrace you as well and hold you to my heart.

(27-32) ***KING DUNCAN.***
Welcome hither:
I have begun to plant thee, and will labour
To make thee full of growing.—Noble Banquo,
That hast no less deserv'd, nor must be known
No less to have done so, let me infold thee
And hold thee to my heart.

(32-33) **BANQUO.**
If I grow in your heart, your majesty, then I'll be growing for the benefit of both myself and you.

(32-33) ***BANQUO.***
There if I grow,
The harvest is your own.

(33-43) **KING DUNCAN.**
All my joys, which I assure you are unrestrained

in their sheer delight, are trying to disguise themselves in my tears.

Sons, lords, friends, all of you who are nearest to me, I here wish to announce that my son Malcolm will inherit the crown when I part from this world.

And I give him the title, effective immediately, of the Prince of Cumberland. But, rest assured, he is not the only one getting a noble title. Because noble titles, like stars, will shine on all that deserve them.

To Macbeth.
Let's head now to your estate, in Inverness, where I suspect we will be going a lot further into your debt, due to all the honours you will undoubtedly pay us as our host, Macbeth.

(33-43) ***KING DUNCAN.***
My plenteous joys,
Wanton in fulness, seek to hide themselves
In drops of sorrow.—Sons, kinsmen, thanes,
And you whose places are the nearest, know,
We will establish our estate upon
Our eldest, Malcolm; whom we name hereafter
The Prince of Cumberland: which honour must
Not unaccompanied invest him only,
But signs of nobleness, like stars, shall shine
On all deservers.—From hence to Inverness,
And bind us further to you.

(44-48) **MACBETH.**
Your majesty, even rest would be tiresome if it were not time dedicated to serving you. I will go on off ahead myself to delight my wife by telling her the happy news of your coming. Farewell.

(44-48) ***MACBETH.***
The rest is labour, which is not us'd for you:
I'll be myself the harbinger, and make joyful
The hearing of my wife with your approach;
So, humbly take my leave.

(48) **KING DUNCAN.**
Our worthy Macbeth!

(48) ***KING DUNCAN.***

My worthy Cawdor!

(49-53) **MACBETH.** *To himself.*
Malcolm Prince of Cumberland! Is he the step on which I will trip and fall, or else can I manage to jump over that obstacle? Yes, in the way of my destiny he lies as a barrier.

Oh, stars, please hide your light so none can see my shady dark desires. And let my eyes not observe what my hands may do. Though what my eyes may fear seeing done, I must do still, or else I may not become king.

Macbeth exits.

(49-53) ***MACBETH.***
Aside:
The Prince of Cumberland!—That is a step
On which I must fall down, or else o'erleap,
For in my way it lies. Stars, hide your fires!
Let not light see my black and deep desires.
The eye wink at the hand, yet let that be,
Which the eye fears, when it is done, to see.

(54-58) **KING DUNCAN.**
You are right, brave Banquo, Macbeth is quite as brilliant as you said. And when he is praised it feeds my own honour too. Today I'm feeding like a glutton at a banquet!

Come on, let's go quickly after him on our horses to his estate, where he's off as quick as he can to prepare our welcome. What a worthy man!

(54-58) ***KING DUNCAN.***
True, worthy Banquo! He is full so valiant;
And in his commendations I am fed.
It is a banquet to me. Let's after him,
Whose care is gone before to bid us welcome:
It is a peerless kinsman.

Trumpets play and all leave to prepare for their departure to Macbeth's castle in Inverness.

ACT ONE

SCENE FIVE

In Inverness, in a room in Macbeth's castle, Lady Macbeth is reading a letter just received from Macbeth.

MODERN TRANSLATION:

ORIGINAL LANGUAGE:

(1-28) **LADY MACBETH.**
'I met them the day I defeated the rebels, and they made some predictions that came true, which suggests they have true psychic knowledge. I was desperate to question them further, but they vanished into the air like spirits.

Whilst I was standing in a trance at the wonder of what they told me, a messenger from the King arrived calling me the 'Lord of Cawdor'. This was also how the witches greeted me, and they also said that I will be king.

I thought it best to tell you of this news, my dearest partner in greatness, so you don't lose any opportunity to rejoice in this information as well. You shouldn't be ignorant of it and the greatness that is promised to both us. Please hold this news to your heart, and farewell.'

You are already the Lord of Glamis and Cawdor, and you will become all else that is promised to you. However, I do doubt your hardness, Macbeth. You are too full of the milk of human kindness, as the poet said, to get what must be done, done. No, I don't doubt you would very much like to be great, and, no, you don't lack for ambition, but what you do lack is the wickedness required to actually undertake the action required.

Yes, you want to be all high and mighty and powerful, yet you also want to be oh so holy. No, you don't want to cheat and lie, but yes, you still want to be king, and by any means possible. What you want, great lord, is someone who tells you that 'you must do this, and you must do that'. To do the things you fear to execute, but would most certainly not regret once having done them.

Come home now, Macbeth, so I can pour some evil spirits in your ears, and thereby persuade you with my tongue to abandon all the doubts that impede you from doing the deed needed to become king. To be king, that thing which fate and all things supernatural do seem already to have anointed you.

A Servant enters.

Yes?

(1-28) ***LADY MACBETH.***

"They met me in the day of success; and I have learned by the perfect'st report they have more in them than mortal knowledge. When I burned in desire to question them further, they made themselves air, into which they vanished. Whiles I stood rapt in the wonder of it, came missives from the King, who all-hailed me, 'Thane of Cawdor'; by which title, before, these Weird Sisters saluted me, and referred me to the coming on of time, with 'Hail, king that shalt be!' This have I thought good to deliver thee (my dearest partner of greatness) that thou might'st not lose the dues of rejoicing, by being ignorant of what greatness is promis'd thee. Lay it to thy heart, and farewell."

Glamis thou art, and Cawdor; and shalt be
What thou art promis'd. Yet do I fear thy nature;
It is too full o' th' milk of human kindness
To catch the nearest way. Thou wouldst be great;
Art not without ambition, but without
The illness should attend it. What thou wouldst highly,

That wouldst thou holily; wouldst not play false,
And yet wouldst wrongly win. Thou'dst have, great Glamis,
That which cries, "Thus thou must do," if thou have it;
And that which rather thou dost fear to do,
Than wishest should be undone. Hie thee hither,
That I may pour my spirits in thine ear,
And chastise with the valour of my tongue
All that impedes thee from the golden round,
Which fate and metaphysical aid doth seem
To have thee crown'd withal.

Enter a Servant.

What is your tidings?

(29) **SERVANT.**
The King comes tonight.

(29) SERVANT.
The King comes here tonight.

(29-31) **LADY MACBETH.**
You are crazy. If the King was coming, wouldn't Macbeth be with him, and if so, wouldn't he have forewarned us of their arrival, in order for us to be able to prepare an appropriate welcome?

LADY MACBETH.
Thou'rt mad to say it.
Is not thy master with him? who, were't so,
Would have inform'd for preparation.

(32-35) **SERVANT.**
Whether you like it or not, my lady, it is true.

But Macbeth is coming first, my friend saw him and then ran back as fast as he could to warn us. Yes, my friend was so out of breath that I could barely understand a word he was saying.

(32-35) SERVANT.
So please you, it is true. Our thane is coming.
One of my fellows had the speed of him,
Who, almost dead for breath, had scarcely more
Than would make up his message.

(35-56) **LADY MACBETH.**
Do give your friend a drink then. He has brought us great news.

The Servant exits.

Just like that bird of ill omen, the raven, the messenger is out of breath, croaking out King Duncan's imminent arrival. Come forth, you evil spirits that deal in death, make a manly man of me. Fill me from my head to my toe with a man's heartless and shameless brutality. Make my blood so thick that it cannot flow as effortlessly to my heart.

Spirits, stop any empathy from flowing from my feminine heart. It will only discourage me from my brutal goal, and disrupt it, and its accomplishment.

Spirits, come to my woman's breasts and take my nursing milk and replace it with poison. Yes, come, you murderous mediating unseen spirits, who aid the grim reaper himself in his mischiefs.

Come, dark night, and engulf yourself in your darkest smoke of hell, so that my sharp dagger cannot see the wounds that it makes. Nor, dark night, let heaven peep through the sky's blanket of darkness to cry 'Stop! No! Stop!'

Macbeth enters.

Great Glamis, courageous Cawdor, greater than both to yet to become, your letters have transported me from indulgent ignorance. I'm now conscious of a fantastical future, that can be easily fulfilled for us in an instant, by one simple act.

(35-56) ***LADY MACBETH.***
Give him tending.
He brings great news.

Exit Servant.

The raven himself is hoarse
That croaks the fatal entrance of Duncan
Under my battlements. Come, you spirits

That tend on mortal thoughts, unsex me here,
And fill me, from the crown to the toe, top-full
Of direst cruelty! make thick my blood,
Stop up th' access and passage to remorse,
That no compunctious visitings of nature
Shake my fell purpose, nor keep peace between
Th' effect and it! Come to my woman's breasts,
And take my milk for gall, your murd'ring ministers,
Wherever in your sightless substances
You wait on nature's mischief! Come, thick night,
And pall thee in the dunnest smoke of hell
That my keen knife see not the wound it makes,
Nor heaven peep through the blanket of the dark
To cry, "Hold, hold!"

Enter Macbeth.

Great Glamis, worthy Cawdor!
Greater than both, by the all-hail hereafter!
Thy letters have transported me beyond
This ignorant present, and I feel now
The future in the instant.

(56-57) **MACBETH.**
My dearest love, Duncan arrives tonight.

(56-57) ***MACBETH.***
My dearest love,
Duncan comes here tonight.

(57) **LADY MACBETH.**
And when will he leave?

(57) ***LADY MACBETH.***
And when goes hence?

(58) **MACBETH.**
He intends to leave tomorrow.

(58) ***MACBETH.***
Tomorrow, as he purposes.

(58-68) **LADY MACBETH.**
A tomorrow that will he will never see. Your face reads like a book, Macbeth. And it's telling me the dull story of a man who feels anxious and disordered.

If you want to deceive, then you must instead look like the occasion requires. Be gregarious in your welcome, your demeanour, and with your words. On the outside, you can look like a little innocent pretty flower, but you can still be a snake underneath, in your heart.

The King is coming, and he must be provided for. You, my dear, you must put the great deeds to be done tonight into my nimble hands. Yes, tonight's deeds, the deeds which will make all nights and days to come ours to rule and command.

(58-68) ***LADY MACBETH.***
O, never
Shall sun that morrow see!
Your face, my thane, is as a book where men
May read strange matters. To beguile the time,
Look like the time; bear welcome in your eye,
Your hand, your tongue: look like the innocent flower,
But be the serpent under't. He that's coming
Must be provided for; and you shall put
This night's great business into my dispatch;
Which shall to all our nights and days to come
Give solely sovereign sway and masterdom.

(69) **MACBETH.**
We will speak more later.

(69) ***MACBETH.***
We will speak further.

(69-71) **LADY MACBETH.**
But ensure you appear clear-eyed and innocent.
If you darken your expression,
It'll just arouse suspicion.
You can leave all the rest to me.

(69-71) ***LADY MACBETH.***
Only look up clear;
To alter favour ever is to fear.
Leave all the rest to me.

Macbeth leaves the room.

ACT ONE

SCENE SIX

In the lush landscape before Macbeth's castle, music plays to welcome King Duncan, Malcolm, Donalbain, Banquo, Lennox, Macduff, Ross, Angus and their attendants, as they arrive on horseback.

MODERN TRANSLATION:

(1-3) **KING DUNCAN.**
This castle has a very pleasant location. The fresh air lightly and sweetly invigorates my senses.

(3-10) **BANQUO.**
This guest of summer here, the martlet, is a bird that builds its nests only upon churches. It has been noted that this bird only congregates and breeds in locations where the air is of the very best quality.

The artful constructions here about prove that heaven's breath does smell most enchantingly here. Indeed, you can see that there is no projection, column, spire or any suitable spot of this church in front of us, in which the martlet has not made its merry nest.

Lady Macbeth arrives to greet them.

ORIGINAL LANGUAGE:

(1-3) ***KING DUNCAN.***
This castle hath a pleasant seat. The air
Nimbly and sweetly recommends itself
Unto our gentle senses.

(3-10) ***BANQUO.***
This guest of summer,
The temple-haunting martlet, does approve,
By his loved mansionry, that the heaven's breath
Smells wooingly here: no jutty, frieze,
Buttress, nor coign of vantage, but this bird
hath made his pendant bed and procreant cradle.
Where they most breed and haunt, I have observ'd
The air is delicate.

Enter Lady Macbeth.

(10-14) **KING DUNCAN.**
Look, look! Our beautiful hostess! I understand that unrequited love often causes a lady trouble, but, the love I feel is genuine love still.

As such, I ask you to ask God directly to forgive me for all the trouble the love I feel may cause to you.

(10-14) ***KING DUNCAN.***
See, see, our honour'd hostess!—
The love that follows us sometime is our trouble,
Which still we thank as love. Herein I teach you
How you shall bid God 'ild us for your pains,
And thank us for your trouble.

(14-20) **LADY MACBETH.**
All the service we do for you, even if it were done twice, and then done double again, it would still be a very poor and trivial compensation for those honours broad and deep that your majesty has brought to our humble home.

We are eternally in your debt for everything you've done for us. We are nothing more than your hermits, your highness.

LADY MACBETH.
All our service,
In every point twice done, and then done double,
Were poor and single business to contend
Against those honours deep and broad wherewith
Your Majesty loads our house: for those of old,
And the late dignities heap'd up to them,
We rest your hermits.

(20-25) **KING DUNCAN.**
Where is the Lord of Cawdor? We chased after him as fast as possible, and had hoped to beat him in arriving here, but he rode much too fast for us.

No doubt, my lady, his great love for you spurred him on to race home as fast was humanly possible. Noble and beautiful lady, we are you honoured guests tonight.

(20-25) KING DUNCAN.
Where's the Thane of Cawdor?
We cours'd him at the heels, and had a purpose
To be his purveyor: but he rides well;
And his great love, sharp as his spur, hath holp him
To his home before us. Fair and noble hostess,
We are your guest tonight.

(25-28) **LADY MACBETH.**
We, your humble servants hoard and save all that we have in safekeeping in order to be able to repay you whenever you ask for it.

Remember, we return what is ours to you, because it is earned only for you, and your admiration. It is, of course, merely on loan to us.

(25-28) LADY MACBETH.
Your servants ever
Have theirs, themselves, and what is theirs, in compt,
To make their audit at your Highness' pleasure,
Still to return your own.

(28-31) **KING DUNCAN.**
Give me your hand, and lead us to our host, Macbeth. We love him, and will forever honour him with our graces.

With your permission, my lady, we will go forth.

(28-31) KING DUNCAN.
Give me your hand;
Conduct me to mine host: we love him highly,
And shall continue our graces towards him.
By your leave, hostess.

They all enter Macbeth's castle gates.

ACT ONE

SCENE SEVEN

Within Macbeth's castle, music is playing, and torches are being lit. A butler enters with servants and they lay out a table in preparation for a feast. Macbeth is standing alone.

MODERN TRANSLATION:

ORIGINAL LANGUAGE:

(1-28) **MACBETH.** *To himself.*
If it only would all be over and done with, once 'it' is done, then it could all be done quickly, and forgotten about.

Yes, if the consequences could be safely locked away, and success were therefore the only possible outcome, then the act itself could be the be-all and the end-all. And no consequences to face at all!

But, no, of course it cannot be so simple. We risk God's judgment. Yes, we inevitably die and we must then face our maker. We are here on earth for a limited time only, but then there is always the eternity to come, is there not?

Also, in a case such as this, we are also likely to face earthly judgements as well. In the first instance, we will be giving a violent example to our enemies, which, once it's taught, will teach them how they could have their wicked revenge upon us. Yes, a revenge with which they could make us taste all the individual ingredients of our plot with our own lips. Yes, and then we too will taste its lethal aftertaste.

Well, the King is here, and he does trust us twice. Firstly, I am his cousin, and secondly, his loyal subject. Both of which, of course, are reasons I should abandon the deed. And, as his host, I should be guarding his door against any intruders of murderous intent, and not hoisting the knife myself.

In addition, this King has been such a good and kind king and has been so guiltless and blameless in his actions, that his virtues are spruiked as if by angels. And their dulcet tones will amplify against the sinful satanic crime of his murder. Pity, like an innocent new-born baby, will blow from the whirlwind triggered by the news. It will be carried as if by angels across the air, by invisible couriers of rumour and fact, so that the vision of our horrific deed will blot every eye. And the tears for Duncan will soak Scotland's soil in a flood.

In all, I have no reason to fulfil my wicked plan except for my bounding ambition, which makes me jump over a hurdle that will probably only land me in an abyss anyway.

Lady Macbeth enters.

What's happened? Any news?

(1-28) ***MACBETH.***

If it were done when 'tis done, then 'twere well
It were done quickly. If th' assassination
Could trammel up the consequence, and catch
With his surcease success; that but this blow
Might be the be-all and the end-all—here,
But here, upon this bank and shoal of time,
We'd jump the life to come. But in these cases
We still have judgement here; that we but teach
Bloody instructions, which being taught, return
To plague th' inventor. This even-handed justice
Commends th' ingredience of our poison'd chalice
To our own lips. He's here in double trust:

First, as I am his kinsman and his subject,
Strong both against the deed; then, as his host,
Who should against his murderer shut the door,
Not bear the knife myself. Besides, this Duncan
Hath borne his faculties so meek, hath been
So clear in his great office, that his virtues
Will plead like angels, trumpet-tongued, against
The deep damnation of his taking-off;
And pity, like a naked new-born babe,
Striding the blast, or heaven's cherubin, hors'd
Upon the sightless couriers of the air,
Shall blow the horrid deed in every eye,
That tears shall drown the wind.—I have no spur
To prick the sides of my intent, but only
Vaulting ambition, which o'erleaps itself
And falls on th' other—

Enter Lady Macbeth.

How now! what news?

(29) **LADY MACBETH.**
He has almost dined. Why did you leave him?

(29) LADY MACBETH.
He has almost supp'd. Why have you left the chamber?

(30) **MACBETH.**
Has he asked for me?

(30) MACBETH.
Hath he ask'd for me?

(30) **LADY MACBETH.**
You know he has!

(30) LADY MACBETH.
Know you not he has?

(31-35) **MACBETH.**
My dear, we cannot continue with our evil plot. He has honoured me only recently, and I have won the plaudits of many distinguished people, golden praises that honour me. And I should wear them gladly, not cast them aside like worthless rags.

(31-35) MACBETH.
We will proceed no further in this business:
He hath honour'd me of late; and I have bought
Golden opinions from all sorts of people,
Which would be worn now in their newest gloss,

Not cast aside so soon.

(35-45) **LADY MACBETH.**
Did you drink up all your ambition when you dressed yourself for tonight? Did you let it get drunk and then fall asleep?

Well, I can tell you that your ambition has now awoken, but it is all hungover, and so sickly and pale, that it is looking completely bewildered at what it had previously so perfectly devised. From now on, as punishment, I will gaze bewilderedly at you, as if a mirror of your wounded ambition.

Are you really afraid to behave toughly and bravely to gain that thing that you desire most in all the world? Would you really rather not have it at all, that thing you do esteem above all else as your life's sole and absolute purpose?

No, you'd be willing to live as a coward in your own knowledge. And let that paltry thought 'I dare not do it' take ascendency over the manly 'do it I will!'?

I fear you're really just a scaredy-cat. Terrified to get your dainty little paws wet, and so allow a delicious, tasty, goldfish to roam far and free, laughing at you mockingly.

(35-45) ***LADY MACBETH.***
Was the hope drunk
Wherein you dress'd yourself? Hath it slept since?
And wakes it now, to look so green and pale
At what it did so freely? From this time
Such I account thy love. Art thou afeard
To be the same in thine own act and valour
As thou art in desire? Wouldst thou have that
Which thou esteem'st the ornament of life,
And live a coward in thine own esteem,
Letting "I dare not" wait upon "I would,"
Like the poor cat i' th' adage?

(45-47) **MACBETH.**
Please! Shut up woman! I am willing to do anything that may honour a man. They who are willing to do more are not real men.

(45-47) ***MACBETH.***
Pr'ythee, peace!
I dare do all that may become a man;
Who dares do more is none.

(47-59) **LADY MACBETH.**
Well, therefore what animal was it that devised this plan for you and gladly revealed it to me so gleefully? No, when you wanted to do it, then you were a man. And an ambition to be all that you can be, to fulfil your potential, well, that makes you so much more of a man, not less.

Listen to me, a suitable time and place didn't present itself before, though you most desperately did want both to contrive themselves. And now destiny has made them both for us, like magic. But this perfect opportunity has just made you doubt it instead of seizing it!

Macbeth, I have breastfed, and I know as a woman, how tenderly you can love that little one that sucks you dearly. But, let me assure you, I would gladly, and while it was smiling at my face mind you, have seized my tit from its boneless gums, and smashed its skull till its baby brain oozed out, if that is what I had sworn on my soul to do. And you, you swore to kill the king!

(47-59) ***LADY MACBETH.***
What beast was't, then,
That made you break this enterprise to me?
When you durst do it, then you were a man;
And, to be more than what you were, you would
Be so much more the man. Nor time nor place
Did then adhere, and yet you would make both:
They have made themselves, and that their fitness now
Does unmake you. I have given suck, and know
How tender 'tis to love the babe that milks me:
I would, while it was smiling in my face,
Have pluck'd my nipple from his boneless gums
And dash'd the brains out, had I so sworn as you
Have done to this.

(59) **MACBETH.**
But what if we fail?

(59) ***MACBETH.***
If we should fail?

(59-72) **LADY MACBETH.**
Then we fail! But if you load some courage and cock the crossbow of fate, then we will not fail.

When Duncan is asleep – and where else would he rather be after his long journey here today than sound asleep in a nice soft warm cosy bed – his two bedroom attendants I will give plenty of wine, merriment and revelry. This will conquer their sense of responsibility no doubt, so that their memory, that safeguard of the mind, and their duty, will vaporise. And along with their reason, all will have dissolved into thin air.

Yes, when he is asleep like a hog in its sty and his consciousness has evaporated all his senses, then he will be as still as if he were dead anyway. And in that state, what act wouldn't we be able to perform to kill him, that poor defenceless, unconscious Duncan? So, what is to impede us from framing his submissive attendants, who will thus bear the guilt entirely for our great victory.

(59-72) ***LADY MACBETH.***
We fail?
But screw your courage to the sticking-place,
And we'll not fail. When Duncan is asleep
(Whereto the rather shall his day's hard journey
Soundly invite him), his two chamberlains
Will I with wine and wassail so convince
That memory, the warder of the brain,
Shall be a fume, and the receipt of reason
A limbeck only: when in swinish sleep
Their drenched natures lie as in a death,
What cannot you and I perform upon
Th' unguarded Duncan? what not put upon
His spongy officers; who shall bear the guilt
Of our great quell?

(72-77) **MACBETH.**
My lady, you must give birth to boys only, for your heroic nature can harvest nothing but males.

Yes, you speak the truth. How can it not be believed, after we have marked his sleepy attendants with their master's blood, that in his bedroom they did use their very own daggers to kill him, and that they are the guilty party?

(72-77) ***MACBETH.***
Bring forth men-children only;
For thy undaunted mettle should compose
Nothing but males. Will it not be receiv'd,
When we have mark'd with blood those sleepy two
Of his own chamber, and us'd their very daggers,
That they have done't?

(77-79) **LADY MACBETH.**
Who could dare to interpret it otherwise, as we make our grief and heartbreak and sorrow roar melodramatically at the news of his passing?

(77-79) ***LADY MACBETH.***
Who dares receive it other,
As we shall make our griefs and clamour roar
Upon his death?

(79-82) **MACBETH.**
I am now settled on the deed. I'll command every reflex of my body to rise to the occasion of this terrible endeavour. Let's go, and we will deceive them all.

Our glad, yielding front will put on a show.
False faces hiding, what false hearts do know.

(79-82) ***MACBETH.***
I am settled, and bend up
Each corporal agent to this terrible feat.
Away, and mock the time with fairest show:
False face must hide what the false heart doth know.

They join their guests for supper.

ACT TWO

SCENE ONE

It is late at night, and within the grounds of Macbeth's castle, Fleance enters with a torch, followed by his father, Banquo.

MODERN TRANSLATION:

(1) **BANQUO.**
What time is it, my son?

(2) **FLEANCE.**
The moon is down. I have not seen a clock.

(3) **BANQUO.**
The moon goes down at midnight.

(3) **FLEANCE.**
I guess it's later than that, father.

(4-9) **BANQUO.**
Take my sword, son.

They must be cost-cutting in heaven, as all their lights are out. Strangely starless sky indeed. Take my armour as well, son.

A heavy weariness, like lead, lies upon me, but yet I still cannot sleep. Morpheus, that god of dreams, I beg you to restrain in me the

ORIGINAL LANGUAGE:

(1) ***BANQUO.***
How goes the night, boy?

(2) ***FLEANCE.***
The moon is down; I have not heard the clock.

(3) ***BANQUO.***
And she goes down at twelve.

(3) ***FLEANCE.***
I take't, 'tis later, sir.

nightmarish thoughts that nature often gives a troubled mind at night.

An unidentifiable man, veiled by the darkness, enters with a servant carrying a torch.

To Fleance.
Hand me my sword.

Who's there?

(4-9) ***BANQUO.***
Hold, take my sword.—There's husbandry in heaven;
Their candles are all out. Take thee that too.
A heavy summons lies like lead upon me,
And yet I would not sleep. Merciful powers,
Restrain in me the cursed thoughts that nature
Gives way to in repose!

Enter Macbeth and a Servant with a torch.

Give me my sword.—Who's there?

(10) **MACBETH.**
A friend.

(10) ***MACBETH.***
A friend.

(11-16) **BANQUO.** *Recognising Macbeth.*
What? Not in bed yet? The king has gone to bed. He has been in an unusually good mood while here, and he has generously bestowed many great gifts upon your household. He even gave your wife a diamond because he said he considers her to be the most delightful hostess he has ever come across. Yes, his stay has been enclosed in unmeasurable levels of satisfaction.

(11-16) ***BANQUO.***
What, sir, not yet at rest? The King's abed:
He hath been in unusual pleasure and
Sent forth great largess to your offices.
This diamond he greets your wife withal,
By the name of most kind hostess, and shut up
In measureless content.

(16-18) **MACBETH.**
We were unprepared for his visit. Therefore, we were unfortunately restricted from the kind of

lavish hospitality we could otherwise have given him.

(16-18) ***MACBETH.***
Being unprepar'd,
Our will became the servant to defect,
Which else should free have wrought.

(18-20) **BANQUO.**
Don't worry about it, Macbeth.

I dreamt last night of the three witches. Some of what they've told you, it has already come true, has it not?

(18-20) ***BANQUO.***
All's well.
I dreamt last night of the three Weird Sisters:
To you they have show'd some truth.

(20-23) **MACBETH.**
Oh, I never think of those witches.

Nonetheless, when we can both find some free time, we should spend that time discussing that business further. That's if you feel that would be time well spent, of course

(20-23) ***MACBETH.***
I think not of them:
Yet, when we can entreat an hour to serve,
We would spend it in some words upon that business,
If you would grant the time.

(23) **BANQUO.**
I'm ready when you are.

(23) ***BANQUO.***
At your kind'st leisure.

(24-25) **MACBETH.**
If you consider what I have to say and think it's well said, then you may well be rewarded with greater honours.

(24-25) ***MACBETH.***
If you shall cleave to my consent, when 'tis,
It shall make honour for you.

(25-28) **BANQUO.**
Only so long as I lose no honour in the pursuit of it. And if my conscience and integrity can also both remain spotless, then I may well be willing to listen to what you may have to tell me.

(25-28) ***BANQUO.***
So I lose none
In seeking to augment it, but still keep
My bosom franchis'd, and allegiance clear,
I shall be counsell'd.

(29) **MACBETH.**
I wish you a good night's sleep, sir.

(29) ***MACBETH.***
Good repose the while!

(30) **BANQUO.**
Thank you. The same to you.

Banquo exits with Fleance.

(30) ***BANQUO.***
Thanks, sir: the like to you.

Exeunt Banquo and Fleance.

(31-64) **MACBETH.** *To the servant.*
Go tell my wife that she must ring the bell when my drink is ready. Then you can go to bed.

The servant exits leaving Macbeth alone.

What's this? A dagger floating before me?

Its handle is drawn to my hand as if by magic. Come, come, let me hold you. Ha! I cannot touch you. Yet I can still see you. Can you only be seen but not held, you instrument of death? Or are you just shaped by my troubled mind, a false hallucination caused by my frenzied thoughts? But see you I most certainly can, and you look as real as me.

You are here to guide me down the path I've already vowed to follow, no doubt. Yes, a weapon just like you, is what I was planning to use. But re my eyes being made a fool of by my mind, or is it the other way around?

I can still see you, you naughty knife. Is that drops of blood on your blade and handle?

No, there is no such thing. Calm down, Macbeth. It is just this bloody business which is deceiving your eyes. It is the dead of night, and all conscious life has descended into wild dreams. Disoriented and deceived by dreams as they gently sleep, witches are making homage to their god, Hecate.

And in the shadows, Murder, withered and old, is awoken by the howls of his wolf, on patrol, on the lookout for victims for his master. And like Tarquin, that legendary rapist, Murder stalks swiftly towards his prey, like a ghost.

The firm earth beneath me, listen not to my steps and pay no attention to the way that I walk. I fear that your hard stones may betray my whereabouts as I walk, which would disturb this dreadful silence. The silence which suits my intentions so aptly of course.

But while I stand here making vain threats, Duncan lives still. Yes, these boasting words only freeze me from my fiery action.

A bell rings.

I'll go, and it will be done. The bell is calling me.

Listen not, Duncan, the toll of this bell,
Rings to send you to heaven, or to hell.

(31-64) ***MACBETH.***
Go bid thy mistress, when my drink is ready,
She strike upon the bell. Get thee to bed.

Exit Servant.

Is this a dagger which I see before me,
The handle toward my hand? Come, let me clutch thee:—
I have thee not, and yet I see thee still.
Art thou not, fatal vision, sensible
To feeling as to sight? or art thou but
A dagger of the mind, a false creation,
Proceeding from the heat-oppressed brain?

I see thee yet, in form as palpable
As this which now I draw.
Thou marshall'st me the way that I was going;
And such an instrument I was to use.
Mine eyes are made the fools o' the other senses,
Or else worth all the rest: I see thee still;
And on thy blade and dudgeon, gouts of blood,
Which was not so before.—There's no such thing.
It is the bloody business which informs
Thus to mine eyes.—Now o'er the one half-world
Nature seems dead, and wicked dreams abuse
The curtain'd sleep. Witchcraft celebrates
Pale Hecate's off'rings; and wither'd murder,
Alarum'd by his sentinel, the wolf,
Whose howl's his watch, thus with his stealthy pace,
With Tarquin's ravishing strides, towards his design
Moves like a ghost.—Thou sure and firm-set earth,
Hear not my steps, which way they walk, for fear
Thy very stones prate of my whereabout,
And take the present horror from the time,
Which now suits with it.—Whiles I threat, he lives.
Words to the heat of deeds too cold breath gives.

A bell rings.

I go, and it is done. The bell invites me.
Hear it not, Duncan, for it is a knell
That summons thee to heaven or to hell.

Macbeth returns inside the castle.

ACT TWO

SCENE TWO

Lady Macbeth is alone in a private room within their castle.

MODERN TRANSLATION:

ORIGINAL LANGUAGE:

(1-8) **LADY MACBETH.**
The drink that's made them drunk, has made me bold. What has placated them, has fired me up. Listen, quiet!

An owl screeching, a broadcaster of death, like the bell that tolls to proclaim a pending execution. Macbeth is getting it done, I'm sure.

The doors to Duncan's room are open, and the drunk servants are making a parody of their responsibilities, by sleeping like dozy babies. I have spiked their milk and wine with drugs galore, so whether they were dead or alive, no one could tell the difference.

(1-8) ***LADY MACBETH.***
That which hath made them drunk hath made me bold:
What hath quench'd them hath given me fire.—
Hark!—Peace!
It was the owl that shriek'd, the fatal bellman,
Which gives the stern'st good night. He is about it.
The doors are open; and the surfeited grooms
Do mock their charge with snores: I have drugg'd their possets,
That death and nature do contend about them,
Whether they live or die.

(8) **MACBETH.** *Heard in an adjacent room.*

Who's there? What's that?

(8) ***MACBETH.***
Within:
Who's there?—what, ho!

(9-13) **LADY MACBETH.**
Damn, have they awoken? With the deed not done? If the act is attempted but not actioned, then we are doomed. Listen!

I laid out the weapons, he could not have missed them. If Duncan didn't look so like my father as he slept, I would gladly have done it myself.

Macbeth enters.

Macbeth!

(9-13) ***LADY MACBETH.***
Alack! I am afraid they have awak'd,
And 'tis not done. Th' attempt and not the deed
Confounds us.—Hark!—I laid their daggers ready;
He could not miss 'em.—Had he not resembled
My father as he slept, I had done't.—My husband!

Enter Macbeth.

(14) **MACBETH.**
The deed is done. You didn't hear a noise?

(14) ***MACBETH.***
I have done the deed.—Didst thou not hear a noise?

(15-16) **LADY MACBETH.**
I heard an owl screech and some crickets cry. Didn't you speak?

(15-16) ***LADY MACBETH.***
I heard the owl scream and the crickets cry.
Did not you speak?

(16) **MACBETH.**
When?

(16) ***MACBETH.***
When?

(16) **LADY MACBETH.**
Now.

(16) ***LADY MACBETH.***
Now.

(16) **MACBETH.**
As I came in?

(16) MACBETH.
As I descended?

(17) **LADY MACBETH.**
Yes.

(17) LADY MACBETH.
Ay.

(17) **MACBETH.**
Listen! – Who's in the second bedroom?

(17) MACBETH.
Hark!—Who lies i' th' second chamber?

(18) **LADY MACBETH.**
Donalbain.

(18) LADY MACBETH.
Donalbain.

(18) **MACBETH.** *Looking at his hands.*
Ah! What a sorry sight.

(18) MACBETH.
This is a sorry sight.

Looking on his hands.

(19) **LADY MACBETH.**
What a foolish thing to say – 'what a sorry sight'.

(19) LADY MACBETH.
A foolish thought, to say a sorry sight.

(20-23) **MACBETH.**
One of his attendants was laughing in his sleep, the other cried 'Murderer!' And they woke each other up. I stopped and listened. But they just said their prayers and settled straight back down to sleep again.

(20-23) MACBETH.
There's one did laugh in's sleep, and one cried, "Murder!"
That they did wake each other: I stood and heard them.
But they did say their prayers, and address'd them
Again to sleep.

(23) **LADY MACBETH.**
There are two lords sleeping in the second bedroom

(23) LADY MACBETH.
There are two lodg'd together.

(24-27) **MACBETH.**
One of his attendants cried 'God bless us' and the other 'Amen', as if they had seen me with my bloody murderer's hands. I heard the fear in their voices, but I couldn't say 'Amen' when they said 'God bless us'.

(24-27) MACBETH.
One cried, "God bless us!" and, "Amen," the other,
As they had seen me with these hangman's hands.
List'ning their fear, I could not say "Amen,"
When they did say, "God bless us."

(28) **LADY MACBETH.**
Don't worry about it.

(28) LADY MACBETH.
Consider it not so deeply.

(29-31) **MACBETH.**
But why couldn't I pronounce 'Amen'? I've never been more in need of a blessing, but the word just stuck in my throat.

(29-31) MACBETH.
But wherefore could not I pronounce "Amen"?
I had most need of blessing, and "Amen"
Stuck in my throat.

(31-32) **LADY MACBETH.**
We mustn't speak of what you've done again. It will only make you crazy.

(31-32) LADY MACBETH.
These deeds must not be thought
After these ways; so, it will make us mad.

(33-38) **MACBETH.**
I thought I heard a voice cry 'Sleep no more, Macbeth is murdering sleep' – the sleep of innocence, the sleep that ties up the tangled ropes of each day's endeavours. Sleep, that passing of each day's life, that bath of recuperative rest from the hard day's labours, that consolation for troubled minds. Sleep, nature's desert in life's great feast.

(33-38) MACBETH.
Methought I heard a voice cry, "Sleep no more!
Macbeth does murder sleep,"—the innocent sleep;
Sleep that knits up the ravell'd sleave of care,
The death of each day's life, sore labour's bath,
Balm of hurt minds, great nature's second course,

Chief nourisher in life's feast.

(38) **LADY MACBETH.**
What are you talking about?

(38) LADY MACBETH.
What do you mean?

(39-41) **MACBETH.**
A voice cried 'sleep no more' to all the house. 'The Lord of Glamis has murdered sleep, and thus Cawdor will sleep no more. Macbeth will sleep no more'.

(39-41) MACBETH.
Still it cried, "Sleep no more!" to all the house:
"Glamis hath murder'd sleep, and therefore Cawdor
Shall sleep no more. Macbeth shall sleep no more!"

(42-48) **LADY MACBETH.**
Who cried these words? Why, great lord, do you want to weaken your noble strength with such insane thoughts?

Now, go and get some water and wash this filthy blood from your hands. And why did you take these knives from the room? They must be found there, you fool. Go, carry them back, and stain the sleeping servants with the blood.

(42-48) LADY MACBETH.
Who was it that thus cried? Why, worthy thane,
You do unbend your noble strength to think
So brainsickly of things. Go get some water,
And wash this filthy witness from your hand.—
Why did you bring these daggers from the place?
They must lie there: go carry them, and smear
The sleepy grooms with blood.

(48-50) **MACBETH.**
I will not go back. I am afraid to think of what I have done. I'd not dare go back into that room for anything.

(48-50) MACBETH.
I'll go no more:
I am afraid to think what I have done;
Look on't again I dare not.

(50-55) **LADY MACBETH.**
Oh! You are pathetic! Give the knives to me then! The sleeping and the dead are just like pictures. And it's only children that find pictures

scary. If Duncan's still bleeding, I'll brush the servants' faces with it, coating them in guilt.

Lady Macbeth exits. Knocking is heard from outside.

(50-55) ***LADY MACBETH.***
Infirm of purpose!
Give me the daggers. The sleeping and the dead
Are but as pictures. 'Tis the eye of childhood
That fears a painted devil. If he do bleed,
I'll gild the faces of the grooms withal,
For it must seem their guilt.

Exit. Knocking within.

(55-61) **MACBETH.**
What is that knocking? What is wrong with me? Any noise astonishes me. Look at these hands! Ha! – these hands that would pluck out my eyes if it meant I could blot out what I've seen. All the water from all the oceans, of all the world couldn't wash this blood off my hands. No, these hands would instead make the endless seas blush, and turn them from blue, to a blood red.

Lady Macbeth re-enters.

(55-61) ***MACBETH.***
Whence is that knocking?
How is't with me, when every noise appals me?
What hands are here? Ha, they pluck out mine eyes!
Will all great Neptune's ocean wash this blood
Clean from my hand? No, this my hand will rather
The multitudinous seas incarnadine,
Making the green one red.

Enter Lady Macbeth.

(62-70) **LADY MACBETH.**
My hands are now the same colour as yours. But never will my blood turn as shamefully cold as yours has.

There is more knocking.

I hear some knocking at the south gate. Let's head to our bedroom. A little water will clean our hands and wash away any guilt. As simple as that! Look at you. Has your courage left you completely?

There is more knocking.

Listen! – more knocking. Go, put on your nightgown. We may be asked if we've seen anything. And in this state, we'll look like we have been up all night long. And abandon all your introspection. It wastes your nerves away.

(62-70) ***LADY MACBETH.***
My hands are of your color, but I shame
To wear a heart so white. Knocking within. I hear knocking
At the south entry:—retire we to our chamber.
A little water clears us of this deed:
How easy is it then! Your constancy
Hath left you unattended.—Knocking within. Hark, more knocking.
Get on your nightgown, lest occasion call us
And show us to be watchers. Be not lost
So poorly in your thoughts.

(71-72) **MACBETH.**
I'd rather be brain-dead, than face up to what I've done.

There is more knocking.

Try and waken Duncan with your knocking, you fool. I wish you could manage that.

(71-72) ***MACBETH.***
To know my deed, 'twere best not know myself.
Knocking within.
Wake Duncan with thy knocking! I would thou couldst!

They go to their bedroom.

ACT TWO

SCENE THREE

Early next morning, before the main gate to Macbeth's castle, there is knocking heard. A porter appears on the inside of the castle gate.

MODERN TRANSLATION:

ORIGINAL LANGUAGE:

(1-20) **THE PORTER.**
Here's a knocker alright! If a man was the porter of hell, he would certainly be kept plenty busy.

There is more knocking.

Knock, knock, knock. Who's there? In Satan's name, welcome to the depths of hell. Maybe it's a farmer? And let's just say he's hanged himself. He'd bought up big and stockpiled all the supplies, but then, oh no, the market collapses and all the demand dies. Good timing mate. You'll need plenty of towels here, sir, for you'll be sweating plenty in the fires of hell for your many sins.

There is more knocking.

Knock, knock. Who's there? In the other devil's name, who's next. By God, here's a conspirator who could argue on opposite sides, for either side, and then both sides still betray. Course he's committed treason enough to offend the Lord, but despite his wiles he couldn't manage to conspire his way up to heaven's door, could he? Oh, come on down, you conspirator you.

There is more knocking.

Knock, knock, knock. Who's there? In God's name, here's an English tailor. What tight pants you have, mate. Nice and dandy! Been skimping on the fabric I see. What madness, skimping on fabric when making baggy trousers, 'a la Francaise'. Come on down tailor. There's plenty of fires here on which you could heat your irons for pressing your trousers.

There is more knocking.

Knock, Knock. Never a moment's rest. Who's this? –

No, this place is too cold to be hell. I'll act the devil's porter no longer. I thought I could've gone through a list of all the professions that go down that old primrose path to self-destruction. Cause a life of selfish pleasure always gets its comeuppance in the everlasting fires of hell, my friend.

There is more knocking.

Hold on! Hold on!

The Porter opens the gate, and Macduff and Lennox enter.

I ask you to treat an old porter with the respect he deserves.

(1-20) ***THE PORTER.***
Here's a knocking indeed! If a man were porter of hell gate, he should have old turning the key.

Knocking.
Knock, knock, knock. Who's there, i' th' name of Belzebub? Here's a farmer that hanged himself on the expectation of plenty: come in time; have napkins enow about you; here you'll sweat for't.

Knocking.

Knock, knock! Who's there, i' th' other devil's name? Faith, here's an equivocator, that could swear in both the scales against either scale, who committed treason enough for God's sake, yet could not equivocate to heaven: O, come in, equivocator.

Knocking.

Knock, knock, knock! Who's there? Faith, here's an English tailor come hither, for stealing out of a French hose: come in, tailor; here you may roast your goose.

Knocking.

Knock, knock. Never at quiet! What are you?—But this place is too cold for hell. I'll devil-porter it no further: I had thought to have let in some of all professions, that go the primrose way to th' everlasting bonfire.

Knocking.

Anon, anon! I pray you, remember the porter.

Opens the gate.

Enter Macduff and Lennox.

(21-22) **MACDUFF.**
Was it so late, my friend, before you went to bed? Why do you sleep so late?

(21-22) ***MACDUFF.***
Was it so late, friend, ere you went to bed,
That you do lie so late?

(23-24) **THE PORTER.**
Well, sir, I was rejoicing till three in the morning and drink, as you surely know, is a great provoker of three things.

(23-24) ***THE PORTER.***
Faith, sir, we were carousing till the second cock; and drink, sir, is a great provoker of three things.

(25) **MACDUFF.**
What three things does drink provoke especially?

(25) ***MACDUFF.***
What three things does drink especially provoke?

(26-33) **THE PORTER.**
For one, sir, it turns your nose red, two, it makes you sleepy, and thirdly, it makes you piss.

But regarding pleasures of the flesh, sir, it both stimulates and stifles. Yes, it stimulates the desire, but it stifles the performance. Therefore, too much drink may be said to be a vacillator with sexual desire: it makes him, and it mars him; it set's him on and puts him off; it encourages him, and disheartens him. It makes him stand tall and erect, but also makes him shrink and shiver up. In conclusion, sir, he'll only end up getting some satisfaction in his sleep. This'll make him lie flat down on his face like a log, where the only climax he'll achieve will be when he comes to wetting his bed at dawn.

(26-33) THE PORTER.
Marry, sir, nose-painting, sleep, and urine. Lechery, sir, it provokes and unprovokes; it provokes the desire, but it takes away the performance. Therefore much drink may be said to be an equivocator with lechery: it makes him, and it mars him; it sets him on, and it takes him off; it persuades him, and disheartens him; makes him stand to, an not stand to; in conclusion, equivocates him in a sleep, and giving him the lie, leaves him.

(34) **MACDUFF.**
Well, I think that too much drink may well have made you lie yourself last night.

(34) MACDUFF.
I believe drink gave thee the lie last night.

(35-37) **THE PORTER.**
That it did, sir, right to my very own face. But I avenged drink for its lies to me, and, I think, me being too strong for it, though it did make me lose my footing a couple of times, I survived to throw it up and spew it out effectively.

(35-37) THE PORTER.
That it did, sir, i' the very throat on me; but I requited him for his lie; and (I think) being too strong for him, though he took up my legs sometime, yet I made a shift to cast him.

(38-39) **MACDUFF.**
Is your master, Macbeth, awake?

Macbeth enters.

It appears our knocking has awoken him. Here he comes.

The Porter leaves.

(38-39) MACDUFF.
Is thy master stirring?

Enter Macbeth.

Our knocking has awak'd him; here he comes.

(40) **LENNOX.**
Good morning, noble Macbeth.

(40) LENNOX.
Good morrow, noble sir!

(40) **MACBETH.**
Good morning to you both.

(40) MACBETH.
Good morrow, both!

(41) **MACDUFF.**
Is the King awake, good lord.

(41) MACDUFF.
Is the King stirring, worthy thane?

(41) **MACBETH.**
Not yet.

(41) MACBETH.
Not yet.

(42-43) **MACDUFF.**
He asked me to arrive early. I fear I'm too late.

(42-43) MACDUFF.
He did command me to call timely on him.
I have almost slipp'd the hour.

(43) **MACBETH.**
I'll take you to him now.

(43) MACBETH.
I'll bring you to him.

(44-45) **MACDUFF.**
I know this is a cheerful chore for you, taking me to see the King, but it is a chore none the less.

(44-45) ***MACDUFF.***
I know this is a joyful trouble to you;
But yet 'tis one.

(46-47) **MACBETH.**
The satisfaction of a duty done defeats any discomfort. Here's his room.

(46-47) ***MACBETH.***
The labour we delight in physics pain.
This is the door.

(47-48) **MACDUFF.**
I'll be so bold as to call in on him alone, for it is a duty expected of me.

Macduff exits.

(47-48) ***MACDUFF.***
I'll make so bold to call.
For 'tis my limited service.

Exit Macduff.

(49) **LENNOX.**
Is the King leaving today?

(49) ***LENNOX.***
Goes the King hence today?

(49) **MACBETH.**
Yes, he did arrange it so.

(49) ***MACBETH.***
He does. He did appoint so.

(50-57) **LENNOX.**
Wasn't the night eerily stormy and otherwise foul? Where I was sleeping, our chimneys were blown down, and crying was heard in the air, strange screams of death. It's said it all foretells, in a most horrific manner, of an appalling era of mayhem and confusion to come, all hatched by this miserable night. The owl, that bird of darkness, in another evil omen, hooted and hollered throughout. And in addition to that, it's said there were earthquakes too.

(50-57) ***LENNOX.***
The night has been unruly: where we lay,
Our chimneys were blown down and, as they say,
Lamentings heard i' th' air, strange screams of death,
And prophesying, with accents terrible,
Of dire combustion and confus'd events,

New hatch'd to the woeful time. The obscure bird
Clamour'd the live-long night. Some say the earth
Was feverous, and did shake.

(57) **MACBETH.**
Well, yes, it was a rough night.

(57) MACBETH.
'Twas a rough night.

(58-59) **LENNOX.**
I may still be but young, however, I cannot recall a night like it before.

Macduff enters.

(58-59) LENNOX.
My young remembrance cannot parallel
A fellow to it.

Enter Macduff.

(59-60) **MACDUFF.**
Ah! Horror of horrors! My tongue nor my heart can understand nor speak of it.

(59-60) MACDUFF.
O horror, horror, horror!
Tongue nor heart cannot conceive nor name thee!

(61) **MACBETH AND LENNOX.**
What's the matter?

(61) MACBETH AND LENNOX.
What's the matter?

(62-65) **MACDUFF.**
Ruin has reached its final climax! A most appalling murder has burst open the temple of our Lord and has stolen all life from within it.

(62-65) MACDUFF.
Confusion now hath made his masterpiece!
Most sacrilegious murder hath broke ope
The Lord's anointed temple, and stole thence
The life o' th' building.

(66) **MACBETH.**
What do you mean, 'all life from within it'?

(66) MACBETH.
What is't you say? the life?

(67) **LENNOX.**
Do you mean the King?

(67) LENNOX.
Mean you his majesty?

(68-77) **MACDUFF.**
Go to his room yourself and defeat your sight with a scene that will turn you to stone. It's Medusa on steroids. Don't ask me to tell you. Go and see it with your own eyes.

Macbeth and Lennox exit.

Wake up! Wake up! Ring the alarms! Murder and treason! Wake up Banquo and Donalbain! Wake up Malcolm! Shake off your drowsy sleep, death's impersonator, and look upon death itself. Wake up, wake up and see a vision of the apocalypse. Malcolm and Banquo, you must rise as if from your graves, and walk like spirits, in order to comprehend the magnitude of this horror.

A bell rings. Lady Macbeth enters.

(68-77) ***MACDUFF.***
Approach the chamber, and destroy your sight
With a new Gorgon. Do not bid me speak.
See, and then speak yourselves.

Exeunt Macbeth and Lennox.

Awake, awake!—
Ring the alarum bell.—Murder and treason!
Banquo and Donalbain! Malcolm! awake!
Shake off this downy sleep, death's counterfeit,
And look on death itself! Up, up, and see
The great doom's image. Malcolm! Banquo!
As from your graves rise up, and walk like sprites
To countenance this horror!

Alarum-bell rings.

Enter Lady Macbeth.

(77-79) **LADY MACBETH.**
What's all this carrying on, with such noisy yelling rousing all the sleepers of my house? Please tell me what's happening.

(77-79) ***LADY MACBETH.***
What's the business,
That such a hideous trumpet calls to parley

The sleepers of the house? Speak, speak!

(79-83) **MACDUFF.**
Oh, gentle lady, it is not for your ears to hear the words that I must utter.

The mere articulation of them in a woman's ear would murder the hearer as soon as they were said.

Banquo enters.

Ah! Banquo, Banquo! Our royal master is murdered!

(79-83) MACDUFF.
O gentle lady,
'Tis not for you to hear what I can speak:
The repetition, in a woman's ear,
Would murder as it fell.

Enter Banquo.

O Banquo, Banquo!
Our royal master's murder'd!

(83-84) **LADY MACBETH.**
Oh, my God! Here, in my house?

(83-84) LADY MACBETH.
Woe, alas!
What, in our house?

(84-86) **BANQUO.**
It'd be too cruel anywhere, madam. My dear Macduff, please make a liar of yourself and say it is not so.

Macbeth, Lennox and Ross enter.

(84-86) BANQUO.
Too cruel anywhere.—
Dear Duff, I pr'ythee, contradict thyself,
And say it is not so.

Enter Macbeth and Lennox with Ross.

(87-92) **MACBETH.**
If I had died only an hour before now, I would've lived a blessed life. For from this moment forward, there is nothing worth living

for. Nothing but triviality. All fame and beauty is dead. The wine of life has spilled. And only a faint residue of its joy is left.

Malcolm and Donalbain enter.

(87-92) ***MACBETH.***
Had I but died an hour before this chance,
I had liv'd a blessed time; for, from this instant
There's nothing serious in mortality.
All is but toys: renown and grace is dead;
The wine of life is drawn, and the mere lees
Is left this vault to brag of.

Enter Malcolm and Donalbain.

(93) **DONALBAIN.**
What? What's happening?

(93) ***DONALBAIN.***
What is amiss?

(94-96) **MACBETH.**
You have been wronged, but do not yet know it. The life spring, the head, the fountain of your bloodline has stopped. Yes, it's been frozen right at its source.

(94-96) ***MACBETH.***
You are, and do not know't:
The spring, the head, the fountain of your blood
Is stopp'd; the very source of it is stopp'd.

(97) **MACDUFF.**
Your royal father has been murdered.

(97) ***MACDUFF.***
Your royal father's murder'd.

(97) **MALCOLM.**
Ah! And by whom?

(97) ***MALCOLM.***
O, by whom?

(98-102) **LENNOX.**
It seems his own attendants did it. Their faces and hands were all covered in blood, and so were their knives, which, soiled with blood, we found on their pillows. The attendants were disorientated and just stared meekly about like imbeciles. We think no man's life could have been trusted anywhere near their hands.

(98-102) ***LENNOX.***

Those of his chamber, as it seem'd, had done't:
Their hands and faces were all badg'd with blood;
So were their daggers, which, unwip'd, we found
Upon their pillows. They star'd, and were distracted;
No man's life was to be trusted with them.

(103-104) **MACBETH.**
And yet, I do feel bad about the fury with which I killed them.

(103-104) ***MACBETH.***
O, yet I do repent me of my fury,
That I did kill them.

(104) **MACDUFF.**
Why did you do that?

(104) ***MACDUFF.***
Wherefore did you so?

(105-115) **MACBETH.**
Who can be both calm and stunned, composed and furious, loyal and impartial, all at the same time? No one can. The speed of my violent act of love made it leap over the hurdle of reason. There lay King Duncan, his silver skin streaked with his golden blood. And his stab wounds looked like ruptures to the natural order, through which destructive devastation would gain admission.

And there stood the murderers, marked with the blood of the King, their knives dressed in slaughter. Who, with a loving heart, could refrain, when faced with such a scene, from revealing the courage in his heart, and announcing to all his love in an act of great passion?

(105-115) ***MACBETH.***
Who can be wise, amaz'd, temperate, and furious,
Loyal and neutral, in a moment? No man:
Th' expedition of my violent love
Outrun the pauser, reason. Here lay Duncan,
His silver skin lac'd with his golden blood;
And his gash'd stabs look'd like a breach in nature
For ruin's wasteful entrance: there, the murderers,
Steep'd in the colours of their trade, their daggers
Unmannerly breech'd with gore. Who could refrain,
That had a heart to love, and in that heart

Courage to make's love known?

(115) **LADY MACBETH.**
Help me! Help me! Please!

Lady Macbeth faints.

*(115) **LADY MACBETH.***
Help me hence, ho!

(116) **MACDUFF.** *To her attendants.*
Go help her.

*(116) **MACDUFF.***
Look to the lady.

(116-117) **MALCOLM.** *To Donalbain only.*
Why do we keep silent, when the question at hand, that of succession to the crown, is ours to claim?

*(116-117) **MALCOLM.***
Why do we hold our tongues,
That most may claim this argument for ours?

(118-120) **DONALBAIN.** *To Malcolm only.*
What can we say, when our fate, now safely concealed, may jump out and seize us madly by surprise? Let's go. Before our tears overcome us.

*(118-120) **DONALBAIN.***
What should be spoken here, where our fate,
Hid in an auger hole, may rush, and seize us?
Let's away. Our tears are not yet brew'd.

(120-121) **MALCOLM.** *To Donalbain only.*
Our deep sorrow has yet to be moved.

*(120-121) **MALCOLM.***
Nor our strong sorrow
Upon the foot of motion.

(121-128) **BANQUO.** *To Lady Macbeth's attendants.*
Go on, help her!

Lady Macbeth is carried out by her attendants.

And when we have composed ourselves, and clothed our naked surprise with poise, let us meet and discuss this most bloody of acts so that we are able to comprehend it in some way.

Wild fears and doubts overwhelm us now. I live to only to honour God, and therefore I will fight with all my might to uncover the secret ambitions which have undoubtedly motivated this treacherous act of hate.

(121-128) ***BANQUO.***
Look to the lady:—

Lady Macbeth is carried out.

And when we have our naked frailties hid,
That suffer in exposure, let us meet,
And question this most bloody piece of work
To know it further. Fears and scruples shake us:
In the great hand of God I stand; and thence
Against the undivulg'd pretence I fight
Of treasonous malice.

(128) **MACDUFF.**
And so will I.

(128) ***MACDUFF.***
And so do I.

(128) **ALL.**
And so will all of us.

(128) ***ALL.***
So all.

(129-130) **MACBETH.**
Let's clothe ourselves with manly determination and meet in the hall.

(129-130) ***MACBETH.***
Let's briefly put on manly readiness,
And meet i' th' hall together.

(130) **ALL.**
Well said.

Everyone exits, except for Malcolm and Donalbain.

(130) ***ALL.***
Well contented.

Exeunt all but Malcolm and Donalbain.

(131-133) **MALCOLM.**
What will you do? I don't think we should associate with these men. It's easier for a charlatan to perform sorrow than it is for a

sincere man to express the real thing. I'll flee to England.

(131-133) ***MALCOLM.***

What will you do? Let's not consort with them:
To show an unfelt sorrow is an office
Which the false man does easy. I'll to England.

(134-137) **DONALBAIN.**

I will go to Ireland. We will each be safer if we take separate paths. Here, the sly conspirators will smile and fawn before stabbing you right in the middle of your back. We are the King's sons. We share his blood. Thus, whoever did this must intend to spill ours, too.

(134-137) ***DONALBAIN.***

To Ireland, I. Our separated fortune
Shall keep us both the safer. Where we are,
There's daggers in men's smiles: the near in blood,
The nearer bloody.

(137-142) **MALCOLM.**

Their murderous plot is loaded and it's only a matter of time before they fire the fatal arrow. We will only survive if we can escape their aim. Therefore, we have no choice but to mount our horses. We cannot make a polite farewell, but must slip away quietly.

It's not a crime for us to steal away,
For we'll get no mercy, if we do stay.

(137-142) ***MALCOLM.***

This murderous shaft that's shot
Hath not yet lighted; and our safest way
Is to avoid the aim. Therefore to horse;
And let us not be dainty of leave-taking,
But shift away. There's warrant in that theft
Which steals itself, when there's no mercy left.

Malcolm and Donalbain depart quietly.

ACT TWO

SCENE FOUR

Outside Macbeth's castle gates, an Old Man and Ross stand together talking. It is daytime, yet strangely dark.

MODERN TRANSLATION:

ORIGINAL LANGUAGE:

(1-4) **OLD MAN.**
I am seventy years old, and I have a good memory still. And throughout all these years, I have seen pass many hours of things both dreadful and strange. But this vile night has made all those seem like nothing in comparison to this night we have just witnessed.

(1-4) ***OLD MAN.***
Threescore and ten I can remember well,
Within the volume of which time I have seen
Hours dreadful and things strange, but this sore night
Hath trifled former knowings.

(4-10) **ROSS.**
Yes, my good man, you can see that the heavens are troubled by what's happened overnight. Look at this foully dark and gloomy sky.

If you go by the clock, it is daytime, but it's as dark as the middle of the night. The sun's extinguished by all the clouds, fog and mists. But is it the supremacy of the night, or the dishonour that the day feels, that hides it? Either way, it allows this unnatural darkness to bury the Earth, at a time when the sun should justly be kissing it.

(4-10) ***ROSS.***

Ha, good father,
Thou seest the heavens, as troubled with man's act,
Threatens his bloody stage: by the clock 'tis day,
And yet dark night strangles the travelling lamp.
Is't night's predominance, or the day's shame,
That darkness does the face of earth entomb,
When living light should kiss it?

(10-13) **OLD MAN.**
Yes, it is as unnatural as the deed that's been done. Listen to this, last Tuesday, a falcon was flying high up in the sky, in its pride of place way up there in the clouds, when I saw an owl, that usually feeds on mice only, fly straight up, seize it, and kill the falcon dead.

(10-13) ***OLD MAN.***
'Tis unnatural,
Even like the deed that's done. On Tuesday last,
A falcon, towering in her pride of place,
Was by a mousing owl hawk'd at and kill'd.

(14-18) **ROSS.**
And likewise with Duncan's horses, a very strange thing indeed happened. His horses are the most beautiful and noble creatures, the darlings of horsekind. And yet, without apparent cause, they went demonic, and broke out of their stalls and went wild. They defied all attempts at obedience, as if they were starting out a war with all of humankind.

(14-18) ***ROSS.***
And Duncan's horses (a thing most strange and certain)
Beauteous and swift, the minions of their race,
Turn'd wild in nature, broke their stalls, flung out,
Contending 'gainst obedience, as they would make
War with mankind.

(18) **OLD MAN.**
I heard it said that they ate each other.

(18) **OLD MAN.**
'Tis said they eat each other.

(19-20) **ROSS.**
Yes, that they did do, to my amazement. Yes, as unbelievable as it was, I did see the horror with my very own eyes.

Macduff enters.

Here comes that good man Macduff.

What is the latest, sir?

(19-20) ***ROSS.***
They did so; to the amazement of mine eyes,
That look'd upon't.
Here comes the good Macduff.

Enter Macduff.

How goes the world, sir, now?

(20-21) **MACDUFF.**
What? Can't you tell from my look?

(20-21) ***MACDUFF.***
Why, see you not?

(21) **ROSS.**
Do you know who murdered the King?

(21) ***ROSS.***
Is't known who did this more than bloody deed?

(22) **MACDUFF.**
The servants that Macbeth killed.

(22) ***MACDUFF.***
Those that Macbeth hath slain.

(23-24) **ROSS.**
Oh, what a terrible day. But what was their motive?

(23-24) ***ROSS.***
Alas, the day!
What good could they pretend?

(24-27) **MACDUFF.**
They were bribed apparently. The King's two sons, Malcolm and Donalbain have fled. Their sudden departure puts all suspicion upon them.

(24-27) ***MACDUFF.***
They were suborn'd.
Malcolm and Donalbain, the King's two sons,
Are stol'n away and fled; which puts upon them
Suspicion of the deed.

(27-30) **ROSS.**
That goes against nature, to kill your own father! Corrupted by a boundless ambition, no doubt, to consume your life's own cause! If this is true, then it is probable that the crown will land on Macbeth's head.

(27-30) ***ROSS.***
'Gainst nature still:
Thriftless ambition, that will ravin up
Thine own life's means!—Then 'tis most like
The sovereignty will fall upon Macbeth.

(31-32) **MACDUFF.**
It has been announced already and they have all gone to Scone to crown him.

(31-32) ***MACDUFF.***
He is already nam'd; and gone to Scone
To be invested.

(33) **ROSS.**
Where's Duncan's body?

(33) ***ROSS.***
Where is Duncan's body?

(34-36) **MACDUFF.**
It's been carried off to Colmekill. That sacred burial ground of Scottish Kings, and the guardian of their bones.

(34-36) ***MACDUFF.***
Carried to Colmekill,
The sacred storehouse of his predecessors,
And guardian of their bones.

(36) **ROSS.**
Are you going to Scone to see him crowned?

(36) ***ROSS.***
Will you to Scone?

(37) **MACDUFF.**
No, cousin, I am going home to Fife.

(37) ***MACDUFF.***
No, cousin, I'll to Fife.

(37) **ROSS.**
I'll go to Scone.

(37) ***ROSS.***
Well, I will thither.

(38-39) **MACDUFF.**
Well, make sure things there are done correctly. Farewell, I fear our old clothes may fit us better than our new ones will.

(38-39) ***MACDUFF.***
Well, may you see things well done there. Adieu!
Lest our old robes sit easier than our new!

(40) **ROSS.**
Farewell, Old Man.

(40) ***ROSS.***
Farewell, father.

(41-42) **OLD MAN.**
God's blessing to you all, and all of those,
Who make good of evil, and friends of foes.

(41-42) ***OLD MAN.***
God's benison go with you; and with those
That would make good of bad, and friends of foes!

The Old Man, Ross and Macduff each depart in their own way.

ACT THREE

SCENE ONE

Banquo is alone in a room in Macbeth's castle.

MODERN TRANSLATION:

ORIGINAL LANGUAGE:

(1-10) **BANQUO.** *To himself.*
You now have it all, Macbeth. You're King, Cawdor and Glamis, just as those three witches promised you. But I fear that you acted most brazen and bad to gain it. However, the witches said that your children would not inherit the crown. No, they said that the succession would fall upon my line, and that I would father many kings. If the witches have told me the truth – as they have told it to you, Macbeth, as their well-fulfilled prophecies show – and if their tales have come true for you, then why shouldn't the oracles speak true for me too.

But quiet, I'll speak no more.

Trumpets play. Macbeth enters as King, Lady Macbeth as Queen, with Lennox, Ross, various lords and attendants.

(1-10) ***BANQUO.***
Thou hast it now, King, Cawdor, Glamis, all,
As the Weird Women promis'd; and, I fear,
Thou play'dst most foully for't; yet it was said
It should not stand in thy posterity;
But that myself should be the root and father
Of many kings. If there come truth from them
(As upon thee, Macbeth, their speeches shine)

Why, by the verities on thee made good,
May they not be my oracles as well,
And set me up in hope? But hush; no more.

Sennet sounded. Enter Macbeth as King, Lady Macbeth as Queen; Lennox, Ross, Lords, and Attendants.

(11) **MACBETH.** *Seeing Banquo.*
Ah! Here is our chief guest.

(11) MACBETH.
Here's our chief guest.

(11-13) **LADY MACBETH.**
If he had been forgotten, then it would've been a gap at our great feast that would've entirely disappointed us all.

(11-13) LADY MACBETH.
If he had been forgotten,
It had been as a gap in our great feast,
And all-thing unbecoming.

(14-15) **MACBETH.** *To Banquo.*
Tonight, we are holding a formal dinner, sir, and we request your attendance.

(14-15) MACBETH.
Tonight we hold a solemn supper, sir,
And I'll request your presence.

(15-18) **BANQUO.**
It is up to your highness to command me to what duties I must fulfil, as I am bound by an unravelable knot to your service. A knot that will be forever tied, I hope.

(15-18) BANQUO.
Let your Highness
Command upon me, to the which my duties
Are with a most indissoluble tie
For ever knit.

(19) **MACBETH.**
Are you going for a horse ride this afternoon?

(19) MACBETH.
Ride you this afternoon?

(20) **BANQUO.**
Yes, my good lord.

(20) BANQUO.
Ay, my good lord.

(21-24) **MACBETH.**
Ah, if you hadn't, we would have asked for your good advice, which has always been well-thought out and insightful, at our meeting today.

But it doesn't matter, we can talk tomorrow. Will you go far on your ride?

(21-24) MACBETH.
We should have else desir'd your good advice
(Which still hath been both grave and prosperous)
In this day's council; but we'll take tomorrow.
Is't far you ride?

(25-28) **BANQUO.**
As far, my lord, as I can travel in the time available between now and dinnertime. But I may need to make myself a night rider, for a dark hour or two, unless my horse can ride faster than I think.

(25-28) BANQUO.
As far, my lord, as will fill up the time
'Twixt this and supper: go not my horse the better,
I must become a borrower of the night,
For a dark hour or twain.

(29) **MACBETH.**
Please ensure you do not miss our dinner.

(29) MACBETH.
Fail not our feast.

(30) **BANQUO.**
I will not, my lord.

(30) BANQUO.
My lord, I will not.

(31-37) **MACBETH.**
I hear that our murderous cousins, Malcolm and Donalbain, are staying one in England, and one in Ireland. Neither has confessed to their crime, but instead they fill the ears of all who will listen with false and scandalous tales.

But more of that tomorrow at our meeting. We have a number of matters to discuss. Go you to your horse, Banquo. Goodbye, until you return tonight. Is Fleance going with you?

(31-37) MACBETH.
We hear our bloody cousins are bestow'd

In England and in Ireland; not confessing
Their cruel parricide, filling their hearers
With strange invention. But of that tomorrow,
When therewithal we shall have cause of state
Craving us jointly. Hie you to horse: adieu,
Till you return at night. Goes Fleance with you?

(38) **BANQUO.**
Yes, my good lord. But time is calling us.

(38) BANQUO.
Ay, my good lord: our time does call upon's.

(39-47) **MACBETH.**
I pray your horses will be both swift and steady of foot, as I entrust the health of both of you to their backs. Farewell.

Banquo exits.

Every man may do as he wishes until seven o'clock tonight. To make your company the more enticing, we will keep to ourselves until dinnertime. Until then, my friends, God bless you all.

All leave except for Macbeth and a servant.

A word with you please, boy. Are those men waiting to see me?

(39-47) MACBETH.
I wish your horses swift and sure of foot;
And so I do commend you to their backs.
Farewell.—

Exit Banquo.

Let every man be master of his time
Till seven at night; to make society
The sweeter welcome, we will keep ourself
Till supper time alone: while then, God be with you.

Exeunt Lady Macbeth, Lords, &c.

Sirrah, a word with you. Attend those men
Our pleasure?

(48) **SERVANT.**
Yes, they are my lord. They are waiting outside the castle gate.

(48) **SERVANT.**
They are, my lord, without the palace gate.

(49-75) **MACBETH.**
Bring them to me.

The servant exits.

To be king is nothing, if not to be a safe king. Our fear of Banquo cuts deep, and in his naturally regal nature reigns a man whom we must fear. He is daring, but added to that he also has a heroic courage, and a wisdom to moderate his heroism so that it is always pursued safely.

It is him alone that I fear. With regards to him, my guardian spirits are enfeebled, as it is said in the history books, that Mark Antony's were by Octavius Caesar's. Banquo did interrupt the witches when they first said that I would be king, and asked them to speak to him instead. Then, they prophesied that he would be father to a long line of kings.

Upon my head, they merely placed an infertile crown, and then in my hand they placed a barren ornamental lance, which will be wrenched from my hands by a bastard, as there will be no son of my own to succeed me.

If this be true, then I have murdered gracious Duncan and besmirched my mind only for the glory of Banquo's sons. For them I have put bitterness in the place of peace in my heart. And only for them will I have given up my eternal soul to damnation. All in order to make them kings! To make the seed of Banquo kings! But rather than let it be so, let fate come into the boxing ring and fight me to the death. Who's there?

The Servant enters with two Murderers.

Boy, go wait at the door until we call you.

The Servant exits. Macbeth speaks to the Murderers.

Wasn't it yesterday that we spoke?

(49-75) ***MACBETH.***
Bring them before us.

Exit Servant.

To be thus is nothing,
But to be safely thus. Our fears in Banquo
Stick deep, and in his royalty of nature
Reigns that which would be fear'd: 'tis much he dares;
And, to that dauntless temper of his mind,
He hath a wisdom that doth guide his valour
To act in safety. There is none but he
Whose being I do fear: and under him
My genius is rebuk'd; as, it is said,
Mark Antony's was by Caesar. He chid the sisters
When first they put the name of king upon me,
And bade them speak to him; then, prophet-like,
They hail'd him father to a line of kings:
Upon my head they plac'd a fruitless crown,
And put a barren sceptre in my gripe,
Thence to be wrench'd with an unlineal hand,
No son of mine succeeding. If't be so,
For Banquo's issue have I fil'd my mind;
For them the gracious Duncan have I murder'd;
Put rancours in the vessel of my peace
Only for them; and mine eternal jewel
Given to the common enemy of man,
To make them kings, the seed of Banquo kings!
Rather than so, come, fate, into the list,
And champion me to th' utterance!—Who's there?—

Enter Servant with two Murderers.

Now go to the door, and stay there till we call.

Exit Servant.

Was it not yesterday we spoke together?

(76) **FIRST MURDERER.**
It was, your highness.

*(76) **FIRST MURDERER.***
It was, so please your Highness.

(76-85) **MACBETH.**
Well then, have you considered what I have asked of you? Please remember that before now it has been solely Banquo that has kept you out of favour with both fortune and fate. Why would you ever think it was me?

I made this clear to you at our last meeting, where we reviewed the evidence, and I proved to you that you have been cheated and frustrated by Banquo alone. And I also showed you the go-betweens he used, and a whole litany of other wrongs, that to any half-wit or lunatic it would clearly say, "it is Banquo that did this to us".

*(76-85) **MACBETH.***
Well then, now
Have you consider'd of my speeches? Know
That it was he, in the times past, which held you
So under fortune, which you thought had been
Our innocent self? This I made good to you
In our last conference, pass'd in probation with you
How you were borne in hand, how cross'd, the instruments,
Who wrought with them, and all things else that might
To half a soul and to a notion craz'd
Say, "Thus did Banquo."

(85) **FIRST MURDERER.**
Yes, you made that clear to us, sir.

*(85) **FIRST MURDERER.***
You made it known to us.

(86-92) **MACBETH.**
That I most certainly did. And I will go even further now, which is why I have arranged our second meeting today.

Is tolerance and forgiveness really so strong in your natures that you can let all these injustices pass meekly by? Are you really such pious Christians that you will pray for this 'good' man and his children? This Banquo that with a heavy hand has thrust you right down to the grave and cursed your families forever?

(86-92) ***MACBETH.***
I did so; and went further, which is now
Our point of second meeting. Do you find
Your patience so predominant in your nature,
That you can let this go? Are you so gospell'd,
To pray for this good man and for his issue,
Whose heavy hand hath bow'd you to the grave,
And beggar'd yours forever?

(92) **FIRST MURDERER.**
We are men, your highness.

(92) ***FIRST MURDERER.***
We are men, my liege.

(93-109) **MACBETH.**
Yes, I can see that you would be listed in the catalogue of men, just as hounds and greyhounds, mongrels, spaniels, retrievers, bulldogs, labradors and mastiffs are listed in the catalogue of dogs.

In that catalogue, the purchase price is distinguished between the swift, the slow, the sensitive, the shrewd, the watchdog, and the hunter. Each one is valued according to what nature has bestowed upon it. Some therefore receive more money than they would from a shop that listed them all at the same price.

And so it is the same with men. Now, so long as are not classified in the catalogue of men as being of the lowest rank, then I will assign the job to you. This job, the execution of which will erase your enemy, and ensure my love and appreciation forever more. I am like a sick man, you see. And Banquo's death will make me well.

You would like to cure me, good sirs?

(93-109) ***MACBETH.***
Ay, in the catalogue ye go for men;
As hounds, and greyhounds, mongrels, spaniels, curs,
Shoughs, water-rugs, and demi-wolves are clept
All by the name of dogs: the valu'd file

Distinguishes the swift, the slow, the subtle,
The housekeeper, the hunter, every one
According to the gift which bounteous nature
Hath in him clos'd; whereby he does receive
Particular addition, from the bill
That writes them all alike: and so of men.
Now, if you have a station in the file,
Not i' th' worst rank of manhood, say't;
And I will put that business in your bosoms,
Whose execution takes your enemy off,
Grapples you to the heart and love of us,
Who wear our health but sickly in his life,
Which in his death were perfect.

(109-112) **SECOND MURDERER.**
Your highness, I am someone who has been so belittled and demeaned by the world, who is so incensed and angry at all the injustices I've faced, that I would have no qualms about doing anything at all that might show my overwhelming spite for all mankind.

(109-112) ***SECOND MURDERER.***
I am one, my liege,
Whom the vile blows and buffets of the world
Hath so incens'd that I am reckless what
I do to spite the world.

(112-115) **FIRST MURDERER.**
Me as well. I am so thoroughly weary of misfortune, and ill-treated by fate, that I would happily risk my life for any chance to either fix it, or end it.

(112-115) ***FIRST MURDERER.***
And I another,
So weary with disasters, tugg'd with fortune,
That I would set my life on any chance,
To mend it or be rid on't.

(115-116) **MACBETH.**
So both of you know that Banquo is your enemy.

(115-116) ***MACBETH.***
Both of you
Know Banquo was your enemy.

(116) **BOTH MURDERERS.**
We do, my lord.

(116) ***BOTH MURDERERS.***

True, my lord.

(117-127) **MACBETH.**
Banquo is my enemy too. I hold him in such a ferocious hatred, that every breath he breathes, suffocates my heart. And although I could easily, with my brutal strength, kill him myself, and be justified in doing so, I cannot.

This is because certain people who are friends of both him and I, whose friendships I must maintain, you see, would weakly bemoan and grumble about me killing him. And therefore, it is such that I must woo your assistance, in order to mask the business from the public view. I won't bore you any longer, but trust me, there are many more dull and weighty reasons for it.

(117-127) MACBETH.
So is he mine; and in such bloody distance,
That every minute of his being thrusts
Against my near'st of life; and though I could
With barefac'd power sweep him from my sight,
And bid my will avouch it, yet I must not,
For certain friends that are both his and mine,
Whose loves I may not drop, but wail his fall
Who I myself struck down: and thence it is
That I to your assistance do make love,
Masking the business from the common eye
For sundry weighty reasons.

(127-128) **SECOND MURDERER.**
We will, my lord, perform the act you ask of us.

(127-128) SECOND MURDERER.
We shall, my lord,
Perform what you command us.

(128) **FIRST MURDERER.**
Though our lives…

(128) FIRST MURDERER.
Though our lives—

(129-140) **MACBETH.** *Interrupting him.*
Your noble spirits shine through you. Before this hour's over, I will advise you where to hide yourselves. I will also give you the exact time and place that the murder should happen. For it

must take place tonight. And it must be done some distance from my castle.

Always keep in mind that I cannot be suspected of plotting this. Also, please do make sure that you do not leave any evidence or botch the job in any way. His son Fleance, who never leaves Banquo's side – his death is as dear to me as that of his father – and he must also face the same fate at the darkly appointed hour. Let's part and resolve ourselves to the deed required on our own. I'll come and get you all shortly.

(129-140) ***MACBETH.***
Your spirits shine through you. Within this hour at most,
I will advise you where to plant yourselves,
Acquaint you with the perfect spy o' th' time,
The moment on't; for't must be done tonight
And something from the palace; always thought
That I require a clearness. And with him
(To leave no rubs nor botches in the work)
Fleance his son, that keeps him company,
Whose absence is no less material to me
Than is his father's, must embrace the fate
Of that dark hour. Resolve yourselves apart.
I'll come to you anon.

(140) **BOTH MURDERERS.**
We are already resolved to it, your highness.

(140) ***BOTH MURDERERS.***
We are resolv'd, my lord.

(141-143) **MACBETH.**
I'll get you shortly. Hide inside.

The Murderers exit.

It is decided. Banquo, tonight your soul leaves your body.

If your soul flies to heaven, or to hell,
Tonight's concluding terminus will tell.

(141-143) ***MACBETH.***
I'll call upon you straight: abide within.

Exeunt Murderers.

It is concluded. Banquo, thy soul's flight,
If it find heaven, must find it out tonight.

Macbeth leaves the room to go see his wife.

ACT THREE

SCENE TWO

In a private room in their castle, Lady Macbeth waits with her servant.

MODERN TRANSLATION:

(1) **LADY MACBETH.**
Has Banquo left the castle?

(2) **HER SERVANT.**
Yes, madam, but he'll return again tonight.

(3-4) **LADY MACBETH.**
Tell the King, my husband, that I would like to speak to him.

(5) **HER SERVANT.**
Yes, madam.

Her Servant exits.

(6-14) **LADY MACBETH.**
Nothing's been gained, and everything's been lost,

ORIGINAL LANGUAGE:

(1) ***LADY MACBETH.***
Is Banquo gone from court?

(2) ***HER SERVANT.***
Ay, madam, but returns again tonight.

(3-4) ***LADY MACBETH.***
Say to the King, I would attend his leisure
For a few words.

(5) ***HER SERVANT.***
Madam, I will.

Exit.

If dreams are attained at too great a cost.
Oh, better to be those whom we destroy,
Than we who lure ruin and lose all joy.

Macbeth enters.

Come now, my love, why do you remain alone, only making friends with your most despairing fantasies. You are not thinking thoughts that should have died off at the same time as those who you worry yourself over are you?

Things which cannot be remedied should not be thought of. What is done, is done.

(6-14) ***LADY MACBETH.***
Naught's had, all's spent,
Where our desire is got without content:
'Tis safer to be that which we destroy,
Than by destruction dwell in doubtful joy.

Enter Macbeth.

How now, my lord, why do you keep alone,
Of sorriest fancies your companions making,
Using those thoughts which should indeed have died
With them they think on? Things without all remedy
Should be without regard: what's done is done.

(15-28) **MACBETH.**
We have only wounded the snake, not killed it. It will heal itself, and its venomous tongue will again threaten us with our guilt. I'd rather the universe fell apart, and heaven and hell were both annihilated, than continue forever to eat our meals in fear, and sleep restlessly in the grip of nightmares that will shudder us night upon night. It would be better if we were with those we killed instead.

Yes, those whom we killed to obtain our great reward, but whom we have instead sent to the peace we now crave. We have trapped our minds in torture chambers, where they now reside in restless turmoil.

But Duncan is safely in his grave. After all the frantic excitements of his life, he now can sleep well. Treason has done the worst that could ever be done to him. He's now safe. Weapons, poisons, domestic fracas and foreign invaders threaten him no more. Nothing can touch him now.

(15-28) ***MACBETH.***
We have scorch'd the snake, not kill'd it.
She'll close, and be herself; whilst our poor malice
Remains in danger of her former tooth.
But let the frame of things disjoint,
Both the worlds suffer,
Ere we will eat our meal in fear, and sleep
In the affliction of these terrible dreams
That shake us nightly. Better be with the dead,
Whom we, to gain our peace, have sent to peace,
Than on the torture of the mind to lie
In restless ecstasy. Duncan is in his grave;
After life's fitful fever he sleeps well;
Treason has done his worst: nor steel, nor poison,
Malice domestic, foreign levy, nothing
Can touch him further.

(28-30) **LADY MACBETH.**
Oh, come on, calm yourself, my love. Brighten up your bleak face. Please do be charming and cheerful amongst our guests tonight.

(28-30) ***LADY MACBETH.***
Come on,
Gently my lord, sleek o'er your rugged looks;
Be bright and jovial among your guests tonight.

(30-36) **MACBETH.**
I will, my love. And I ask you to perform the same act. Remember to flirt with Banquo, gift him your presence, flatter him with your eye and tongue. We are not safe if we are not loved, so we must deceive and make ourselves look good and honourable by flattering all and sundry. Let's make our faces masks, which conceal what is truly within our hearts.

(30-36) ***MACBETH.***
So shall I, love; and so, I pray, be you.
Let your remembrance apply to Banquo;
Present him eminence, both with eye and tongue:

Unsafe the while, that we
Must lave our honours in these flattering streams,
And make our faces vizards to our hearts,
Disguising what they are.

(36) **LADY MACBETH.**
Oh, you must stop all this talk.

(36) ***LADY MACBETH.***
You must leave this.

(37-38) **MACBETH.**
My mind is full of demons, dear wife. You know as well as I that Banquo and Fleance still live.

(37-38) ***MACBETH.***
O, full of scorpions is my mind, dear wife!
Thou know'st that Banquo, and his Fleance, lives.

(39) **LADY MACBETH.**
But their lease on life is not eternal.

(39) ***LADY MACBETH.***
But in them nature's copy's not eterne.

(40-45) **MACBETH.**
There is some comfort in that, they are mortal. So I'll be glad then. Before the bat has flown his nocturnal flight. Before the goddess of the night, Hectate, summons the dung beetle, with its evening hum that signifies it's time for rest, another deadly deed will be done.

(40-45) ***MACBETH.***
There's comfort yet; they are assailable.
Then be thou jocund. Ere the bat hath flown
His cloister'd flight, ere to black Hecate's summons
The shard-born beetle, with his drowsy hums,
Hath rung night's yawning peal, there shall be done
A deed of dreadful note.

(45) **LADY MACBETH.**
What will be done?

(45) ***LADY MACBETH.***
What's to be done?

(46-57) **MACBETH.**
You don't need to know, my dear, until you're able to applaud the outcome. Come on night, seal up and blindfold the tender eyes of daytime. And with your deadly and invisible hands, eliminate and tear Banquo to pieces!

He whose beating heart keeps me white with fright all of the night. The light of day is muddying, and the crow is flying off to the woods to feed. The bright things of the daytime are beginning to droop and drowse to sleep, whilst the dark creatures of the night begin to rouse. I can see that you wonder at my words, but hush, my dear.

We can repair our reign with just one more Bad deed done. Now follow me through this door.

(46-57) ***MACBETH.***

Be innocent of the knowledge, dearest chuck,
Till thou applaud the deed. Come, seeling night,
Scarf up the tender eye of pitiful day,
And with thy bloody and invisible hand
Cancel and tear to pieces that great bond
Which keeps me pale!—Light thickens; and the crow
Makes wing to th' rooky wood.
Good things of day begin to droop and drowse,
Whiles night's black agents to their preys do rouse.
Thou marvell'st at my words: but hold thee still;
Things bad begun make strong themselves by ill.
So, pr'ythee, go with me.

They exit to the dining room, entering the banquet.

ACT THREE

SCENE THREE

Near a gate leading to the castle, three Murderers stand waiting in the murky dusk.

MODERN TRANSLATION:

ORIGINAL LANGUAGE:

(1) **FIRST MURDERER.** *To the Third Murderer.*
But who asked you to join us?

*(1) **FIRST MURDERER.***
But who did bid thee join with us?

(2) **THIRD MURDERER.**
Macbeth.

*(2) **THIRD MURDERER.***
Macbeth.

(3-4) **SECOND MURDERER.** *To the First Murderer.*
I think we can trust him. He knows all details about what we must do and how we must do it. Therefore, Macbeth must've told him.

*(3-4) **SECOND MURDERER.***
He needs not our mistrust; since he delivers
Our offices and what we have to do
To the direction just.

(4-8) **FIRST MURDERER.** *To the Third Murderer.*
Join us, then. The west still glimmers with some streaks of daylight. A late guest would be quickening to arrive before nightfall, no doubt. Our victim is surely coming near, my friends.

*(4-8) **FIRST MURDERER.***

Then stand with us.
The west yet glimmers with some streaks of day.
Now spurs the lated traveller apace,
To gain the timely inn; and near approaches
The subject of our watch.

(8) **THIRD MURDERER.**
Quiet, I hear horses.

(8) THIRD MURDERER.
Hark! I hear horses.

(9) **BANQUO.** *From a distance.*
Give me a light, please.

(9) BANQUO.
Within.
Give us a light there, ho!

(9-11) **SECOND MURDERER.**
This is him. All the other expected guests have arrived already.

(9-11) SECOND MURDERER.
Then 'tis he; the rest
That are within the note of expectation
Already are i' th' court.

(11) **FIRST MURDERER.**
Listen, his horses are being led to the stable.

(11) FIRST MURDERER.
His horses go about.

(12-14) **THIRD MURDERER.**
It's almost a mile to the castle gate. And as most men do, he usually walks the distance.

Banquo and Fleance enter, with a torch, unable to see their murderers.

(12-14) THIRD MURDERER.
Almost a mile; but he does usually,
So all men do, from hence to the palace gate
Make it their walk.

Enter Banquo and Fleance with a torch.

(14) **SECOND MURDERER.** *To the other Murderers.*
A light, a light.

(14) SECOND MURDERER.
A light, a light!

(14) **THIRD MURDERER.** *To the other Murderers.*

It is him.

(14) ***THIRD MURDERER.***
'Tis he.

(15) **FIRST MURDERER.** *To the other Murderers.*
Let's do it.

(15) ***FIRST MURDERER.***
Stand to't.

(16) **BANQUO.**
It looks like it will rain tonight.

(16) ***BANQUO.***
It will be rain tonight.

(16) **FIRST MURDERER.**
Then let it rain down upon you, sir.

The First Murderer puts out the torch, and the other Murderers attack Banquo.

(16) ***FIRST MURDERER.***
Let it come down.

Assaults Banquo.

(17-18) **BANQUO.**
Ah! betrayal! Run, good Fleance, run, run, run!
You may avenge me later – Oh, you villains!

Banquo dies, and Fleance flees.

(17-18) ***BANQUO.***
O, treachery! Fly, good Fleance, fly, fly, fly!
Thou mayst revenge—O slave!

Dies. Fleance escapes.

(19) **THIRD MURDERER.**
Who put out the torch?

(19) ***THIRD MURDERER.***
Who did strike out the light?

(20) **FIRST MURDERER.**
Why leave it lit?

(20) ***FIRST MURDERER.***
Was't not the way?

(21) **THIRD MURDERER.**
We've only gotten one of them. The son's fled.

(21) ***THIRD MURDERER.***
There's but one down: the son is fled.

(22) **SECOND MURDERER.**
We've missed the main target.

(22) SECOND MURDERER.
We have lost best half of our affair.

(23) **FIRST MURDERER.**
Well, can't do much about it now, let's go and report on what we've done to Macbeth.

(23) FIRST MURDERER.
Well, let's away, and say how much is done.

The Murderers exit with Banquo's corpse.

ACT THREE

SCENE FOUR

A banquet is being held in a grand room of Macbeth's castle. Macbeth enters as King, Lady Macbeth as Queen. Ross, Lennox, other lords and various attendants are awaiting them, standing about the room.

MODERN TRANSLATION:

ORIGINAL LANGUAGE:

(1-2) **MACBETH.**
You all know your correct seats. Please sit down. To one and all, a hearty welcome.

(1-2) ***MACBETH.***
You know your own degrees, sit down. At first
And last the hearty welcome.

(2) **THE LORDS.**
Thank you your majesty.

The Lords sit down.

(2) ***THE LORDS.***
Thanks to your Majesty.

(3-5) **MACBETH.**
Don't fear, I will mingle with you all, and act the gregarious host. My wife waits at the head of the table, but in good time I'll request that she welcomes you all here.

(3-5) ***MACBETH.***
Ourself will mingle with society,
And play the humble host.
Our hostess keeps her state; but, in best time,
We will require her welcome.

(6-7) **LADY MACBETH.** *Sitting at the table.*
Say it for me, sir. My heart is simply beating their welcome.

The First Murderer stands at the door.

(6-7) LADY MACBETH.
Pronounce it for me, sir, to all our friends;
For my heart speaks they are welcome.

Enter first Murderer to the door.

(8-11) **MACBETH.**
See, they answer you in their hearts only too, so we're even.

He moves himself to the periphery of the guests.

I'll stand near you all here. Please don't restrain your enjoyment. To start, we'll all drink a shot of whiskey.

They all down a shot and Macbeth moves towards the door and speaks to the First Murderer.

I see there's blood on your face.

(8-11) MACBETH.
See, they encounter thee with their hearts' thanks.
Both sides are even: here I'll sit i' th' midst.

Be large in mirth; anon we'll drink a measure
The table round. There's blood upon thy face.

(12) **FIRST MURDERER.** *To Macbeth.*
It must be Banquo's then.

(12) FIRST MURDERER.
'Tis Banquo's then.

(13-14) **MACBETH.**
Better on you than in him. Is he eliminated?

(13-14) MACBETH.
'Tis better thee without than he within.
Is he dispatch'd?

(15) **FIRST MURDERER.**
My lord, his throat is cut. I did that for him.

(15) **FIRST MURDERER.**
My lord, his throat is cut. That I did for him.

(16-18) **MACBETH.**
You are the best of the cutthroats. But let's not overlook him that did the same to Fleance. If that were you too, then you are a cutthroat extraordinaire.

(16-18) MACBETH.
Thou art the best o' th' cut-throats;
Yet he's good that did the like for Fleance:
If thou didst it, thou art the nonpareil.

(18-19) **FIRST MURDERER.**
Sir, Fleance escaped.

(18-19) **FIRST MURDERER.**
Most royal sir,
Fleance is 'scap'd.

(20-24) **MACBETH.**
Here comes my madness again. It all would've been perfect, as flawless as marble, as solid as rock, as free and liberated as the air around us. But as it is, I am trapped, restricted, imprisoned, and entwined in unrelenting doubts and fears.

But Banquo's safely dispatched?

(20-24) MACBETH.
Then comes my fit again: I had else been perfect;
Whole as the marble, founded as the rock,
As broad and general as the casing air:
But now I am cabin'd, cribb'd, confin'd, bound in
To saucy doubts and fears. But Banquo's safe?

(25-27) **FIRST MURDERER.**
Yes, my good lord. He is safely dispatched to a ditch, with twenty cavernous wounds to his head. Just one of them would've been enough to kill him.

(25-27) FIRST MURDERER.
Ay, my good lord. Safe in a ditch he bides,
With twenty trenched gashes on his head;
The least a death to nature.

(27-31) **MACBETH.**
Well, thank you for that. So the snake is slain. The worm his son has escaped and will become venomous for revenge in time, no doubt, but he doesn't have the teeth yet to worry us.

Go, leave me, sir. Tomorrow we'll meet again.

The First Murderer exits.

(27-31) ***MACBETH.***
Thanks for that.
There the grown serpent lies; the worm that's fled
Hath nature that in time will venom breed,
No teeth for th' present.—Get thee gone; tomorrow
We'll hear, ourselves, again.

Exit Murderer.

(31-36) **LADY MACBETH.**
My royal lord, you are not playing the part of the charming host. If you're not ensuring that the ambience is entertaining and hospitable, then they'll feel more like customers at an inn than welcomed and honoured guests. If you are merely eating for the sake of eating, then you may as well be at home. But when you're eating out, the hospitality is the icing on the cake. Gatherings are surely dull without it.

Banquo's Ghost appears unnoticed and sits in Macbeth's allotted seat at the table.

(31-36) ***LADY MACBETH.***
My royal lord,
You do not give the cheer: the feast is sold
That is not often vouch'd, while 'tis a-making,
'Tis given with welcome. To feed were best at home;
From thence the sauce to meat is ceremony;
Meeting were bare without it.

The Ghost of Banquo rises, and sits in Macbeth's place.

(36-38) **MACBETH.**
Ah, my sweet, you prompt me correctly. For good digestion, you require a good meal, and for good health, you need both!

(36-38) ***MACBETH.***
Sweet remembrancer!—
Now, good digestion wait on appetite,
And health on both!

(38) **LENNOX.**
Would it please you to sit down, your highness.

(38) ***LENNOX.***

May't please your Highness sit.

(39-42) **MACBETH.**
We would have all of Scotland's nobility here tonight, if only the righteous Banquo were present. I'd rather think him a rude and disrespectful so and so, than imagine that he's met some misfortune on his way here.

(39-42) MACBETH.
Here had we now our country's honour roof'd,
Were the grac'd person of our Banquo present;
Who may I rather challenge for unkindness
Than pity for mischance!

(42-44) **ROSS.**
His absence, sir, merely suggests that he made a false promise. Please, your highness, sit down and grace us who are here with your presence.

(42-44) ROSS.
His absence, sir,
Lays blame upon his promise. Please't your Highness
To grace us with your royal company?

(45) **MACBETH.**
But the table's full.

(45) MACBETH.
The table's full.

(45) **LENNOX.**
Your seat is reserved, sir.

(45) LENNOX.
Here is a place reserv'd, sir.

(46) **MACBETH.**
Where?

(46) MACBETH.
Where?

(47) **LENNOX.**
Here, my lord. What's the matter, your highness?

(47) LENNOX.
Here, my good lord. What is't that moves your Highness?

(48) **MACBETH.**
Which of you has done this?

(48) MACBETH.
Which of you have done this?

(48) **THE LORDS.**
Done what, my lord?

(48) THE LORDS.
What, my good lord?

(49-50) **MACBETH.** *To Banquo's Ghost.*
You cannot say that I did it. Do not shake your ghastly hair at me.

(49-50) MACBETH.
Thou canst not say I did it. Never shake
Thy gory locks at me.

(51) **ROSS.** *Standing.*
Arise gentleman. His highness is unwell.

(51) ROSS.
Gentlemen, rise; his Highness is not well.

(52-57) **LADY MACBETH.** *Standing.*
Please, sit down, my friends. My lord often acts like this. And he has done so since a child. I beg you, please take your seats. His fits are only temporary. In a moment, he will be all well again. If you take too much notice of this outburst, you will simply offend him and prolong it unnecessarily. Please, continue eating and pay him no attention.

She speaks to Macbeth.

What, are you a man or a mouse?

(52-57) LADY MACBETH.
Sit, worthy friends. My lord is often thus,
And hath been from his youth: pray you, keep seat;
The fit is momentary; upon a thought
He will again be well. If much you note him,
You shall offend him, and extend his passion.
Feed, and regard him not.—Are you a man?

(58-59) **MACBETH.**
A man, and a brave one I must be, if I can allow myself to gaze on things which would terrify the devil himself.

(58-59) MACBETH.
Ay, and a bold one, that dare look on that
Which might appal the devil.

(59-67) **LADY MACBETH.**
Oh, what nonsense! This truly is the very embodiment of your fear. It's that floating, painted dagger again, isn't it? You told me all about how it led you to Duncan.

Oh, your fits and starts. It's simply sham anxiety, I say, and not real fear. Such prattle would only suit a schoolgirl's ghost story, and should only scare her grandma! Oh, this is shameful. Why do you look so terrified? At the end of the day, when all's said and done, you are looking on nothing but an unoccupied chair!

(59-67) ***LADY MACBETH.***
O proper stuff!
This is the very painting of your fear:
This is the air-drawn dagger which you said,
Led you to Duncan. O, these flaws, and starts
(Impostors to true fear), would well become
A woman's story at a winter's fire,
Authoris'd by her grandam. Shame itself!
Why do you make such faces? When all's done,
You look but on a stool.

(68-72) **MACBETH.**
Please, can't you see? Please, look! Wait – it speaks! Oh, why should I care? If you can nod your head, why not speak as well! If our morgues and graveyards only send our dead straight back to us, then why not just let scavenging birds eat the carcasses instead. The birdies' guts can be their tombs.

Banquo's Ghost disappears.

(68-72) ***MACBETH.***
Pr'ythee, see there!
Behold! look! lo! how say you?
Why, what care I? If thou canst nod, speak too.—
If charnel houses and our graves must send
Those that we bury back, our monuments
Shall be the maws of kites.

Ghost disappears.

(72) **LADY MACBETH.**
What, have you not made enough of a fool of yourself? You cannot call yourself a man!

(72) ***LADY MACBETH.***
What, quite unmann'd in folly?

(73) **MACBETH.**
As I stand here, he sat there.

(73) ***MACBETH.***
If I stand here, I saw him.

(73) **LADY MACBETH.**
My god! You are shameless!

(73) ***LADY MACBETH.***
Fie, for shame!

(74-82) **MACBETH.**
Ah! Blood has been shed before. In the old days, before law and order took hold, bloodshed was quite commonplace. Yes, and even since, murders still happen, murders too horrific to bear listening to.

But, in the past, when brains were battered, men would die, and that would be the end of that. Now, it seems, men rise again, and even with twenty wounds stabbed into their skulls, they have the gall to sit in our chairs and steal our places at the dinner table! And this, I swear, is much more transgressive than any act of murder ever was.

(74-82) ***MACBETH.***
Blood hath been shed ere now, i' th' olden time,
Ere humane statute purg'd the gentle weal;
Ay, and since too, murders have been perform'd
Too terrible for the ear: the time has been,
That, when the brains were out, the man would die,
And there an end; but now they rise again,
With twenty mortal murders on their crowns,
And push us from our stools. This is more strange
Than such a murder is.

(82-83) **LADY MACBETH.** *To the whole room.*
Please, my lord, remember that your noble friends are here.

(82-83) ***LADY MACBETH.***
My worthy lord,
Your noble friends do lack you.

(83-91) **MACBETH.**
I do beg your pardon. Do not be alarmed by me, my most worthy friends. I have a strange disorder, I'm afraid, which is a nuisance, but does not bother those that know me well. I will make a toast, to wish love and health to all. And

then I'll sit down.

Come, waiter, give me some wine. Fill it right to the brim. Let's drink to the general joy and well-being of the whole table. And to our dear friend Banquo, whom we all miss. I really do wish he were here with us. So, to him and to all, let's raise our glasses.

To good love and good health!

(83-91) ***MACBETH.***
I do forget.—
Do not muse at me, my most worthy friends.
I have a strange infirmity, which is nothing
To those that know me. Come, love and health to all;
Then I'll sit down.—Give me some wine, fill full.—
I drink to the general joy o' th' whole table,
And to our dear friend Banquo, whom we miss:
Would he were here.

Ghost rises again.

To all, and him, we thirst,
And all to all.

(91) **THE LORDS.**
To good love and good health.

They all drink. Banquo's Ghost returns.

(91) ***THE LORDS.***
Our duties, and the pledge.

(92-95) **MACBETH.**
Away, and out of my sight! Hide in the earth where you belong. Your bones have no marrow! Your blood is cold! And your eyes can't see, yet you glare at me still.

(92-95) ***MACBETH.***
Avaunt! and quit my sight! let the earth hide thee!
Thy bones are marrowless, thy blood is cold;
Thou hast no speculation in those eyes
Which thou dost glare with!

(95-97) **LADY MACBETH.**
My good friends, look on this as nothing but an old habit. It is nothing more. Even though it may dim our pleasures a tad.

(95-97) LADY MACBETH.
Think of this, good peers,
But as a thing of custom: 'tis no other,
Only it spoils the pleasure of the time.

(98-107) **MACBETH.**
What any man dares to do, I'll do. If you came to me like a rugged Russian bear, or a horned Rhinoceros, or a Caspian tiger, or any creature other than yourself, my firm muscles would not tremble. Or if you came alive again, and you dared to challenge me with your sword, I'd not blink an eye. If I trembled then, you'd be justified in calling me a scared little baby girl.

But, you, you hideous ghost, depart! Away you mocking hallucination! Out of my sight!

Banquo's ghost disappears.

And, it having gone, I am a man again. Please be seated.

(98-107) MACBETH.
What man dare, I dare:
Approach thou like the rugged Russian bear,
The arm'd rhinoceros, or th' Hyrcan tiger;
Take any shape but that, and my firm nerves
Shall never tremble: or be alive again,
And dare me to the desert with thy sword;
If trembling I inhabit then, protest me
The baby of a girl. Hence, horrible shadow!
Unreal mock'ry, hence!

Ghost disappears.

Why, so;—being gone,
I am a man again.—Pray you, sit still.

(108-109) **LADY MACBETH.**
You have ruined our amusement, and our party, with your outrageous illness.

(108-109) LADY MACBETH.
You have displaced the mirth, broke the good meeting
With most admir'd disorder.

(109-115) **MACBETH.**
Can such things happen and pass us by, like a

summer's cloud, without causing us to notice, and ponder its meaning? You're all making me feel like I'm not the brave man I've always supposed I was. How can one look at such strange sights, and maintain the colour in their cheeks? As you can see, mine have naturally gone white with fear.

(109-115) ***MACBETH.***
Can such things be,
And overcome us like a summer's cloud,
Without our special wonder? You make me strange
Even to the disposition that I owe,
When now I think you can behold such sights,
And keep the natural ruby of your cheeks,
When mine are blanch'd with fear.

(115) **ROSS.**
What sights, my lord?

(115) ***ROSS.***
What sights, my lord?

(116-119) **LADY MACBETH.**
Please, don't speak to him. He'll just get worse and worse. Your talk will only aggravate his disorder, I'm afraid. Please, go home. Don't bother with formally departing in accordance to the order dictated by conventions. Just go. Just go all at once. Go now, I beg you.

(116-119) ***LADY MACBETH.***
I pray you, speak not; he grows worse and worse;
Question enrages him. At once, good night:—
Stand not upon the order of your going,
But go at once.

(119-120) **LENNOX.**
Good night, my lady, and I hope his majesty feels better soon.

(119-120) ***LENNOX.***
Good night; and better health
Attend his Majesty!

(120) **LADY MACBETH.**
I wish a good night to you all.

All lords, and attendants, exit the banquet room.

(120) ***LADY MACBETH.***
A kind good night to all!

Exeunt all Lords and Attendants.

(121-125) **MACBETH.**
They say that bloody deeds will have their revenge. Bloodshed will be avenged by bloodshed. Stones have been seen to walk, and trees to speak. Omens and their meanings have been revealed by magpies, crows and other birds, in order to expose murderers, both guilty and hidden.

What time is it?

(121-125) ***MACBETH.***
It will have blood, they say, blood will have blood.
Stones have been known to move, and trees to speak;
Augurs, and understood relations, have
By magot-pies, and choughs, and rooks, brought forth
The secret'st man of blood.—What is the night?

(126) **LADY MACBETH.**
It's that time when it's hard to tell whether it is late at night or early in the morning.

(126) ***LADY MACBETH.***
Almost at odds with morning, which is which.

(127-128) **MACBETH.**
What do you think of Macduff not wanting to see me?

(127-128) ***MACBETH.***
How say'st thou, that Macduff denies his person
At our great bidding?

(128) **LADY MACBETH.**
Did you ask him to?

(128) ***LADY MACBETH.***
Did you send to him, sir?

(129-139) **MACBETH.**
It's just a rumour I've heard.

But I will send for Macduff, anyway, and see if he accepts. I have infiltrated his homes by paying a servant to inform on him in each of them. And I will go tomorrow, and very early tomorrow, to see the witches. I will ask them for more detailed prophecies, because I'm determined to know the worst that can happen to me.

And for my own good, all other matters will be postponed. I am so mired in blood that retreating backward would be as tricky as continuing on headfirst. I have strange plans in my head, that must be put into action by my hands. But I don't have time to ponder their value.

(129-139) ***MACBETH.***
I hear it by the way; but I will send.
There's not a one of them but in his house
I keep a servant fee'd. I will tomorrow
(And betimes I will) to the Weird Sisters:
More shall they speak; for now I am bent to know,
By the worst means, the worst. For mine own good,
All causes shall give way: I am in blood
Stepp'd in so far that, should I wade no more,
Returning were as tedious as go o'er.
Strange things I have in head, that will to hand,
Which must be acted ere they may be scann'd.

(140) **LADY MACBETH.**
You need that restorer of all men, sleep.

(140) ***LADY MACBETH.***
You lack the season of all natures, sleep.

(141-143) **MACBETH.**
Come, we'll go to bed. My anxiety and self-delusions are just the spawn of these unfamiliar anxieties.

Our life'd been too easy, contented times.
My love, we're still young novices in crimes.

(141-143) ***MACBETH.***
Come, we'll to sleep. My strange and self-abuse
Is the initiate fear that wants hard use.
We are yet but young in deed.

They exit the banquet hall to their private rooms.

ACT THREE

SCENE FIVE

The three Witches and Hecate are waiting in a dark, stormy and desolate field. There is the sound of thunder and rain.

MODERN TRANSLATION:

ORIGINAL LANGUAGE:

(1) **FIRST WITCH.**
Why, what's the matter Hecate? You look angry?

(1) ***FIRST WITCH.***
Why, how now, Hecate? you look angerly.

(2-33) **HECATE.**
Of course, you witches, as you lacked good care,
Too sassy and bold, how'd you dare
To engage with that fool Macbeth,
In riddles and affairs of death.
And I, the monarch of your charms,
The secret plotter of all harms,
Was never asked to play my part
And act out the cream of our art?
And, what is worse, all you have done
Has been for an ungrateful son,
Nasty and angry, who, like others do,
Loves only himself, and not one of you.

But now make amends. Leave my sight
And meet in the morn, not tonight,
In the dark pits of hell, where he
Will come to know his destiny.
Your jugs and spells will deliver,
Your charms and all you require.
I'll fade into air, and tonight

I'll scheme his end with all my might.
This all must be done before noon.
Something will happen to the moon,
It will fall in an act profound,
But I will catch it, not the ground.
This exploit made by magic hands,
Every hobgoblin understands,
And by the power of this trick
Macbeth will become very brain sick.
He will spurn fate, scorn death, and bear
His hopes towards wisdom, not fear.
And we all know false security
Is a mortal's chief enemy.

(2-33) ***HECATE.***

Have I not reason, beldams as you are,
Saucy and overbold? How did you dare
To trade and traffic with Macbeth
In riddles and affairs of death;
And I, the mistress of your charms,
The close contriver of all harms,
Was never call'd to bear my part,
Or show the glory of our art?
And, which is worse, all you have done
Hath been but for a wayward son,
Spiteful and wrathful; who, as others do,
Loves for his own ends, not for you.
But make amends now: get you gone,
And at the pit of Acheron
Meet me i' th' morning: thither he
Will come to know his destiny.
Your vessels and your spells provide,
Your charms, and everything beside.
I am for th' air; this night I'll spend
Unto a dismal and a fatal end.
Great business must be wrought ere noon.
Upon the corner of the moon
There hangs a vap'rous drop profound;
I'll catch it ere it come to ground:
And that, distill'd by magic sleights,
Shall raise such artificial sprites,
As, by the strength of their illusion,
Shall draw him on to his confusion.
He shall spurn fate, scorn death, and bear
His hopes 'bove wisdom, grace, and fear.
And you all know, security

Is mortals' chiefest enemy.

(34-35) **THE SPIRITS.** *Singing from the air.*
Come away, come away.
Hecate, Hecate, come away.

*(34-35) **THE SPIRITS.***
Come away, come away;
Hecate, Hecate, come away.

(36-37) **HECATE.**
Listen, my little spirits do call me,
They sit in the clouds and await, you see.

*(36-37) **HECATE.***
Hark! I am called! My little spirit, see;
Sits in foggy cloud and stays for me.

(38-39) **THE SPIRITS.** *Singing from the air.*
Come away, come away.
Hecate, Hecate, come away.

*(38-39) **THE SPIRITS.***
Come away, come away;
Hecate, Hecate, come away.

(40-43) **HECATE.**
I come, I come, I come, I come.
With all the speed I can,
With all the speed I can,
Where's Stadlin?

*(40-43) **HECATE.***
I come, I come, I come, I come;
With all th' speed I may,
With all th' speed I may.
Where's Stadlin?

(43) **A SPIRIT.**
Here.

*(43) **A SPIRIT.***
Here.

(43) **HECATE.**
Where's Puckle?

*(43) **HECATE.***
Where's Puckle?

(43) **ANOTHER SPIRIT.**
Here.

*(43) **ANOTHER SPIRIT.***
Here.

(44-46) **OTHER SPIRITS.**
And Hoppo, too, and Hellwain, too.

We only lack you, we only lack you.
Come away, away, join us in the sky.

(44-46) ***OTHER SPIRITS.***
And Hoppo, too, and Hellwain, too.
We lack but you, we lack but you.
Come away; make up the count.

(47) **HECATE.**
Anoint me first, and then I will fly.

The spirits appear above Hecate, whilst a spirit that looks like a cat descends.

(47) ***HECATE.***
I will but 'noint, and then I mount.

(48-51) **THE SPIRITS.**
There's one that comes to pay his dues,
A kiss, a hug, a sip of blood.
Why do you wait so long I muse,
The air, the smell, so sweet, so good.

(48-51) ***THE SPIRITS.***
There's one comes down to fetch his dues,
A kiss, a coll, a sip of blood.
Why do thou stay'st so long; I muse, I muse,
Since th' air's so sweet and good.

(52) **HECATE.**
You come for me? What news, what news?

(52) ***HECATE.***
O art thou come? What news, what news?

(53-54) **SPIRIT LIKE A CAT.**
Either you come or you refuse.
Either way it's still our delight.

(53-54) ***SPIRIT LIKE A CAT.***
All goes still to our delight;
Either come, or else refuse, refuse.

(55-57) **HECATE.**
Now I am ready for the flight.

Hecate flies up to the Spirits, and sings.

Now I can go, now I can fly,
Malkin my sweet spirit and I.

(55-57) ***HECATE.***
Now I am furnished for the flight.
Now I go; now I fly,
Malkin my sweet spirit and I.

(58-69) **THE SPIRITS AND HECATE.**
Oh, what a pretty pleasure it is
To ride in the air,
When the moon shines fair.
And sing, and dance, and play and kiss.
Over woods and rocks and mountains,
Over seas and misty fountains.
Over spires, towers and turrets,
We fly by night amongst the spirits,
No rings of bells, no noisy sounds,
No howls of wolves, no barks of hounds.
No, not the noise of waves roaring,
Nor slingshots can us reach soaring.

(58-69) THE SPIRITS AND HECATE.
Oh, what a dainty pleasure 'tis
To ride in th' air
When th' moon shines fair;
And sing, and dance, and toy, and kiss.
Over woods, high rocks and mountains,
Over seas and misty fountains.
Over steeples, towers and turrets,
We fly by night 'mongst troops of spirits.
No ring of bells to our ear sounds;
No howls of wolves, no yelps of hounds;
No, not th' noise of waters-breach
Or cannon's throat our height can reach.

(70-73) **THE SPIRITS**. *In the air.*
No rings of bells, no noisy sounds,
No howls of wolves, no barks of hounds.
No, not the noise of waves roaring,
Nor slingshots can us reach soaring.

Hecate and all the Spirits fly away into the sky.

(70-73) THE SPIRITS.
No ring of bells to our ear sounds;
No howls of wolves, no yelps of hounds;
No, not th' noise of waters-breach,
Or cannon's throat our height can reach.

(74) **FIRST WITCH.**
Come, let's be quick. She'll soon be back again.

(74) FIRST WITCH.
Come, let's make haste; she'll soon be back again.

The Witches vanish into the air.

ACT THREE

SCENE SIX

In a room in Duncan's former castle in Forres, Lennox and another lord sit in deep discussion.

MODERN TRANSLATION:

ORIGINAL LANGUAGE:

(1-24) **LENNOX.**
What I've said previously has mirrored your own opinions. And you can draw your own conclusions as well as I. All I want to say to you is that things have transpired in a very strange manner. The good Duncan was only pitied by Macbeth once he was safely dead. And the same with the brave and heroic Banquo, who was out walking too late at night, I suppose. Well, if it please you, sir you could say that it was Fleance that killed him, since, after all, it was Fleance who fled straight after. And perhaps you could say that men should not be out walking late at night…

And again, who cannot help thinking how monstrous it was for Malcolm and Donalbain to kill their very own kind father? Yes, that damnable deed, oh how it did grieve Macbeth so! Wasn't it also true that he went directly in honest anger to the offending servants, who were the sleepy slaves of drink, and nobly avenge Duncan's death?

Yes, and wisely too, for it would have certainly angered anyone forced to listen to their blundering denials. So, yes, I would say that Macbeth has behaved very much to his advantage, and I think that had he had Duncan's sons under lock and key – as, God willing, he will not – they would soon find out what happens to you if you murder your father. And so too would Fleance.

But I must speak no further, for Macduff made ill-considered remarks, and failed to attend the tyrant's dinner party, and now, I hear, Macduff lives in disgrace. Sir, can you please tell me where Macduff is now staying?

(1-24) ***LENNOX.***
My former speeches have but hit your thoughts,
Which can interpret farther: only, I say,
Thing's have been strangely borne. The gracious Duncan
Was pitied of Macbeth:—marry, he was dead:—
And the right valiant Banquo walk'd too late;
Whom, you may say, if't please you, Fleance kill'd,
For Fleance fled. Men must not walk too late.
Who cannot want the thought, how monstrous
It was for Malcolm and for Donalbain
To kill their gracious father? damned fact!
How it did grieve Macbeth! did he not straight,
In pious rage, the two delinquents tear
That were the slaves of drink and thralls of sleep?
Was not that nobly done? Ay, and wisely too;
For 'twould have anger'd any heart alive,
To hear the men deny't. So that, I say,
He has borne all things well: and I do think,
That had he Duncan's sons under his key
(As, and't please heaven, he shall not) they should find
What 'twere to kill a father; so should Fleance.
But, peace!—for from broad words, and 'cause he fail'd
His presence at the tyrant's feast, I hear,
Macduff lives in disgrace. Sir, can you tell
Where he bestows himself?

(24-39) **A LORD.**
Malcolm, the son of Duncan, from whom Macbeth blocks his rightful claim to the Scottish crown, is currently in the court of the English King, the virtuous King Edward. He pays no heed to Malcolm's misfortunes, and holds him in the highest respect.

Macduff too, has gone to the English court, and petitions King Edward to assist in persuading the Earl of Northumberland, Siward, and his son, to come to our aid.

By the help of these – and if God is willing – we may once more be able to eat well, and sleep well, and ensure our ceremonies and feasts are uncontaminated by malicious plots and bloody knives. Finally, our court would no longer be dishonoured by corrupt powers at play.

But unfortunately, news of these machinations have reached Macbeth directly, who is so infuriated that he is now making preparations for war.

(24-39) ***A LORD.***
The son of Duncan,
From whom this tyrant holds the due of birth,
Lives in the English court and is receiv'd
Of the most pious Edward with such grace
That the malevolence of fortune nothing
Takes from his high respect. Thither Macduff
Is gone to pray the holy king, upon his aid
To wake Northumberland, and warlike Siward
That, by the help of these (with Him above
To ratify the work), we may again
Give to our tables meat, sleep to our nights;
Free from our feasts and banquets bloody knives,
Do faithful homage, and receive free honours,
All which we pine for now. And this report
Hath so exasperate the King that he
Prepares for some attempt of war.

(40) **LENNOX.**
Did he send for Macduff's help?

(40) ***LENNOX.***
Sent he to Macduff?

(41-44) **A LORD.**
Macbeth sent a messenger to him. Macduff replied with a stern 'No, not I'. The messenger's countenance darkened, and he haughtily turned his head and rudely proceeded to hum a dim tune, as if to say, 'you'll rue the day you

lumbered me with having to do the duty of giving such an answer to Macbeth'.

(41-44) ***A LORD.***
He did: and with an absolute "Sir, not I,"
The cloudy messenger turns me his back,
And hums, as who should say, "You'll rue the time
That clogs me with this answer."

(44-50) **LENNOX.**
Hmm, but such arrogance from his underlings may warn Macduff that he needs to be cautious, and keep far away. Certainly, if it didn't, I would have to question his wisdom.

But I do, nonetheless, wish an angel could fly off to the English court and implore him to return immediately, as Scotland is suffering so without him.

(44-50) ***LENNOX.***
And that well might
Advise him to a caution, t' hold what distance
His wisdom can provide. Some holy angel
Fly to the court of England, and unfold
His message ere he come, that a swift blessing
May soon return to this our suffering country
Under a hand accurs'd!

(50) **A LORD.**
If I could, I'd send my prayers along with that angel in a heartbeat.

(50) **A LORD.**
I'll send my prayers with him.

Lennox and the Lord conclude their discussion. Lennox takes his leave to return to Macbeth's castle in Inverness.

ACT FOUR

SCENE ONE

Three Witches gather around a cauldron boiling over fire, in a dark cave, surrounded by animal, and other, corpses. Once again, there is the sound of thunder and rain.

MODERN TRANSLATION:

(1) **FIRST WITCH.**
Three times the brown cat has meowed.

(2) **SECOND WITCH.**
Three times plus one the hedgehog's whined.

(3) **THIRD WITCH.**
My own owl, Harpier, cries, 'it's time, it's time'.

(4-9) **FIRST WITCH.**
Round about our black cauldron go,
The poisoned bowels within we'll throw,
The toad that under a cold stone,
Days and nights rests near thirty-one,
Its deadly venom forms all hot
And we'll boil it first in our pot.

ORIGINAL LANGUAGE:

(1) ***FIRST WITCH.***
Thrice the brinded cat hath mew'd.

(2) ***SECOND WITCH.***
Thrice, and once the hedge-pig whin'd.

(3) ***THIRD WITCH.***
Harpier cries:—'Tis time, 'tis time.

(4-9) ***FIRST WITCH.***
Round about the cauldron go;
In the poison'd entrails throw.—
Toad, that under cold stone
Days and nights has thirty-one
Swelter'd venom sleeping got,

Boil thou first i' th' charmed pot!

(10-11) **ALL.**
Double, double, toil and trouble,
Fire burn and cauldron bubble.

(10-11) ALL.
Double, double, toil and trouble;
Fire, burn; and cauldron, bubble.

(12-19) **SECOND WITCH.**
A slice of a slimy swamp snake,
In the cauldron, we'll boil and bake.
Eye of lizard, and toe of frog,
Wool of a bat, and tongue of dog,
Snake's tongue too, and a blind-worm's sting
Lizard's leg and baby owl's wing.
All a stew of potent trouble,
Inferno's soup, boil and bubble.

(12-19) SECOND WITCH.
Fillet of a fenny snake,
In the cauldron boil and bake;
Eye of newt, and toe of frog,
Wool of bat, and tongue of dog,
Adder's fork, and blind-worm's sting,
Lizard's leg, and howlet's wing,
For a charm of powerful trouble,
Like a hell-broth boil and bubble.

(20-21) **ALL.**
Double, double, toil and trouble,
Fire burn and cauldron bubble.

(20-21) ALL.
Double, double, toil and trouble;
Fire, burn; and cauldron, bubble.

(22-34) **THIRD WITCH.**
Skin of dragon, a wolf's tooth,
Witches' corpse, the innards with proof,
It's of belly of greedy shark,
Poison hemlock, dug in the dark,
Liver of a blasphemous Jew,
Gallbladder of goat, twigs of yew,
Reaped in view of the moon's eclipse.
Nose of a Turk, and Tartar's lips,
Finger of a strangled baby,
Born by whore in a ditch gloomy,
Ensure the soup's thick and gloopy.
Add to that tiger's intestine

Tada, here is a lethal poison.

(22-34) ***THIRD WITCH.***
Scale of dragon, tooth of wolf,
Witch's mummy, maw and gulf
Of the ravin'd salt-sea shark,
Root of hemlock digg'd i' th' dark,
Liver of blaspheming Jew,
Gall of goat, and slips of yew
Sliver'd in the moon's eclipse,
Nose of Turk, and Tartar's lips,
Finger of birth-strangled babe
Ditch-deliver'd by a drab,
Make the gruel thick and slab:
Add thereto a tiger's chaudron,
For th' ingredients of our cauldron.

(35-36) **ALL.**
Double, double, toil and trouble,
Fire burn and cauldron bubble.

(35-36) ***ALL.***
Double, double, toil and trouble;
Fire, burn; and cauldron, bubble.

(37-38) **SECOND WITCH.**
Then cool it with a baboon's blood
And our potion is set and good.

Hecate enters with three more Witches.

(37-38) ***SECOND WITCH.***
Cool it with a baboon's blood.
Then the charm is firm and good.

Enter Hecate and three other witches.

(39-45) **HECATE.**
Oh, well done! I praise your action,
We shall all have satisfaction.
And now about the cauldron sing,
Like elves and fairies in a ring,
Enchanting all that you put in.

To music and singing.
Black spirits and white, red spirits and grey,
Mingle, mingle, mingle, you that mingle may.

(39-45) ***HECATE.***
O, well done! I commend your pains,
And everyone shall share i' th' gains.

And now about the cauldron sing,
Like elves and fairies in a ring,
Enchanting all that you put in.
Black spirits and white, red spirits and grey,
Mingle, mingle, mingle, you that mingle may.

(46-48) **FOURTH WITCH.**
Titty, Tiffin, keep stiffen'en;
Firedrake, Puckey, make it lucky.
Liard, Robin, you can jump in.

(46-48) FOURTH WITCH.
Titty, Tiffin, keep stiff in;
Firedrake, Puckey, make it lucky.
Liard, Robin, you must bob in.

(49-50) **ALL.**
Around, around, around, about, about,
Let evil run in, all good can stay out.

(49-50) ALL.
Round, around, around, about, about;
An ill come running in, all good keep out.

(51) **FOURTH WITCH.**
Here's the blood of a bat.

(51) FOURTH WITCH.
Here's th' blood of a bat.

(52) **HECATE.**
Put in that, oh, put in that.

(52) HECATE.
Put in that, O, put in that!

(53) **FIFTH WITCH.**
Here's a buttercup.

(53) FIFTH WITCH.
Here's leopard's bane.

(54) **HECATE.**
Put in a scrap.

(54) HECATE.
Put in a grain.

(55) **FOURTH WITCH.**
The juice of toad, the oil of snake.

(55) FOURTH WITCH.
Th' juice of toad, th' oil of adder.

(56) **FIFTH WITCH.**
Those will make the hipster's head ache.

(56) FIFTH WITCH.
Those will make th' younker madder.

(57) **HECATE.**
Put in, all in, and mask the stink.

(57) HECATE.
Put in, there's all, and rid th' stench.

(58) **SIXTH WITCH.**
An ounce of a blonde girl, you think?

(58) SIXTH WITCH.
Nay, here's three ounces of a red-haired wench.

(59-60) **ALL.**
Around, around, around, about, about,
Let evil run in, all good can stay out.

(59-60) ALL.
Round, around, around, about, about;
An ill come running in, all good keep out.

(61-63) **SECOND WITCH.**
I feel some tingling in my thumb.
A thing frightful does this way come.

Knocking is heard.

Open locks, whoever knocks.

Macbeth enters.

(61-63) SECOND WITCH.
By the pricking of my thumbs,
Something wicked this way comes.
Open, locks,
Whoever knocks!

Enter Macbeth.

(64) **MACBETH.**
What's this, you mysterious, murky, nocturnal hags? What are you doing?

(64) MACBETH.
How now, you secret, black, and midnight hags!
What is't you do?

(65) **ALL.**
A deed without a name.

(65) ALL.
A deed without a name.

(66-77) **MACBETH.**
I summon you by the same magic that you practice. By whatever means you know the future, I beg you to answer me with it. Even if it

means you must muster the four winds and blowdown churches, and make the frothy waves uprise and swallow up the ships, and tear up the ripe wheat and blow the forests down, and topple castles upon their sentinels, and turn palaces and pyramids upside down to their foundations, and destroy all the riches of our lush gardens, I don't care. I just care that you answer me what I ask of you.

(66-77) ***MACBETH.***
I conjure you, by that which you profess,
(Howe'er you come to know it) answer me:
Though you untie the winds, and let them fight
Against the churches; though the yesty waves
Confound and swallow navigation up;
Though bladed corn be lodg'd, and trees blown down;
Though castles topple on their warders' heads;
Though palaces and pyramids do slope
Their heads to their foundations; though the treasure
Of nature's germens tumble all together,
Even till destruction sicken, answer me
To what I ask you.

(77) **FIRST WITCH.**
Speak.

(77) ***FIRST WITCH.***
Speak.

(77) **SECOND WITCH.**
Demand.

(77) ***SECOND WITCH.***
Demand.

(77) **THIRD WITCH.**
We'll answer.

(77) ***THIRD WITCH.***
We'll answer.

(78-79) **FIRST WITCH.**
Tell us if you'd rather hear it from our mouths or our masters'.

(78-79) ***FIRST WITCH.***
Say, if thou'dst rather hear it from our mouths,
Or from our masters?

(79) **MACBETH.**
Call your masters. Let me see them.

(79) ***MACBETH.***
Call 'em, let me see 'em.

(83) **FIRST WITCH.**
Pour in pig's blood that's been gobbling
Her nine babies; fat that's dripping
From a murderer on the gallow,
Throw in the flame

(83) ***FIRST WITCH.***
Pour in sow's blood, that hath eaten
Her nine farrow; grease that's sweaten
From the murderer's gibbet throw
Into the flame.

(83-84) **ALL.**
From high or low,
Yourself and role most deftly show.

Thunder sounds and an apparition with an armoured head rises.

(83-84) ***ALL.***
Come, high or low;
Thyself and office deftly show!

Thunder. An Apparition of an armed head rises.

(85) **MACBETH.**
Tell me, you mysterious power…

(85) ***MACBETH.***
Tell me, thou unknown power,—

(85-86) **FIRST WITCH.**
He can hear your thoughts if quiet,
Listen to speech, but stay silent,

(85-86) ***FIRST WITCH.***
He knows thy thought:
Hear his speech, but say thou naught.

(87-88) **FIRST APPARITION.**
Macbeth, Macbeth, Macbeth, beware Macduff.
Beware the Lord of Fife. Away. Enough.

The apparition descends.

(87-88) ***FIRST APPARITION.***
Macbeth! Macbeth! Macbeth! Beware Macduff;
Beware the Thane of Fife.—Dismiss me.—Enough.

Descends.

(89-90) **MACBETH.**
Whatever you are, I thank you for your words

of caution. You have correctly guessed my fears.
But one more question…

(89-90) ***MACBETH.***
Whate'er thou art, for thy good caution, thanks;
Thou hast harp'd my fear aright.—But one word more.

(91-92) **FIRST WITCH.**
He no longer can be summoned.
Here's another more determined.

Thunder sounds and an apparition of a bloody child rises.

(91-92) ***FIRST WITCH.***
He will not be commanded. Here's another,
More potent than the first.

Thunder. An Apparition of a bloody child rises.

(93) **SECOND APPARITION.**
Macbeth, Macbeth, Macbeth.

(93) ***SECOND APPARITION.***
Macbeth! Macbeth! Macbeth!

(94) **MACBETH.**
If I had three ears, then I'd understand you.

(94) ***MACBETH.***
Had I three ears, I'd hear thee.

(95-97) **SECOND APPARITION.**
Be bloody, bold and firm. And laugh with scorn
At man's power, as none of woman born
Will harm Macbeth.

The apparition descends.

(95-97) ***SECOND APPARITION.***
Be bloody, bold, and resolute. Laugh to scorn
The power of man, for none of woman born
Shall harm Macbeth.

Descends.

(98-105) **MACBETH.**
Then live on, Macduff, what reason have I to fear you? But still, to make myself doubly sure of the assurance, I will ensure my fate is secure by murdering you too. Just to be safe and to calm my unmanly fears, and sleep soundly even if there's thunder ranging about me when skies could be clear.

Thunder sounds and an apparition of a crowned child with a branch in its hand rises.

What is this that rises before me, dressed like a king, and wears upon his baby's head the round crown of the monarch?

(98-105) ***MACBETH.***
Then live, Macduff: what need I fear of thee?
But yet I'll make assurance double sure,
And take a bond of fate. Thou shalt not live;
That I may tell pale-hearted fear it lies,
And sleep in spite of thunder.

Thunder. An Apparition of a child crowned, with a tree in his hand, rises.

What is this,
That rises like the issue of a king,
And wears upon his baby brow the round
And top of sovereignty?

(105) **ALL.**
Listen, but don't speak to it.

(105) ***ALL.***
Listen, but speak not to't.

(106-110) **THIRD APPARITION.**
Be lion-hearted, proud and take no care
Who vexes, who irks, or where schemers are.
Macbeth will never be vanquished until
Birnam Wood walks and climbs up that great hill
Dunsinane against him.

The apparition descends.

(106-110) ***THIRD APPARITION.***
Be lion-mettled, proud, and take no care
Who chafes, who frets, or where conspirers are:
Macbeth shall never vanquish'd be, until
Great Birnam wood to high Dunsinane hill
Shall come against him.

Descends.

(110-119) **MACBETH.**
How can that be?

Who can move the forest, and shift a tree,
Whilst it's rooted to earth? Sweet omen good!
No rebel army can surge, till the wood,
Of Birnam rise, and in his role Macbeth
Will strive and live out the lease of his breath
As mortals commonly do. But my heart
Throbs to know one thing. Tell me, if your art
Can forecast this, will Banquo's kids ever
Reign over Scotland?

(110-119) ***MACBETH.***
That will never be:
Who can impress the forest; bid the tree
Unfix his earth-bound root? Sweet bodements, good!
Rebellious head, rise never till the wood
Of Birnam rise, and our high-plac'd Macbeth
Shall live the lease of nature, pay his breath
To time and mortal custom.—Yet my heart
Throbs to know one thing: tell me, if your art
Can tell so much, shall Banquo's issue ever
Reign in this kingdom?

(119) **ALL.**
Seek to know no more.

(119) ***ALL.***
Seek to know no more.

(120-122) **MACBETH.**
I will not be silenced! If you deny me, I will
curse you for all eternity. Tell me now!

The cauldron sinks and music plays.

Why has the cauldron sunk? And what is this
music?

(120-122) ***MACBETH.***
I will be satisfied: deny me this,
And an eternal curse fall on you! Let me know.
Why sinks that cauldron? and what noise is this?

Hautboys.

(123) **FIRST WITCH.**
Show

(123) ***FIRST WITCH.***
Show!

(124) **SECOND WITCH.**
Show

(124) ***SECOND WITCH.***
Show!

(125) **THIRD WITCH.**
Show

(125) ***THIRD WITCH.***
Show!

(126-127) **ALL.**
Show his eyes and grieve his heart,
Come like shadows, then depart.

Banquo's Ghost enters, with a parade of eight kings, the last of them holding a mirror in its hands.

(126-127) ***ALL.***
Show his eyes, and grieve his heart;
Come like shadows, so depart!

A show of eight kings appear, and pass over in order, the last with a glass in his hand; Banquo following.

(128-140) **MACBETH.**
You look too like Banquo. Away!

And this one, your crown sears my eyeballs. And you, your hair is golden like a crown, just the same as the other. And the next one, this king looks the same still.

You filthy hags! Why do you show me this?

And a fourth? My eyes swell at the sight! What, will this line of kings stretch to Armageddon? And another? And a seventh? I can't look anymore. And yet an eighth appears! And he carries a mirror, that shows me more, and more, and more still!

Some I see even have the crests of both Scotland and England, combined in union! What despicable sights! Now I see it is true, that bloody haired Banquo smiles at me, meaning those unionists are all his descendants.

The kings and Banquo's Ghost depart.

So is this what comes?

(128-140) ***MACBETH.***
Thou are too like the spirit of Banquo. Down!
Thy crown does sear mine eyeballs:—and thy hair,
Thou other gold-bound brow, is like the first.
A third is like the former.—Filthy hags!
Why do you show me this?—A fourth!—Start, eyes!
What, will the line stretch out to th' crack of doom?
Another yet!—A seventh!—I'll see no more:—
And yet the eighth appears, who bears a glass
Which shows me many more; and some I see
That twofold balls and treble sceptres carry.
Horrible sight!—Now I see 'tis true;
For the blood-bolter'd Banquo smiles upon me,
And points at them for his.—What! is this so?

(141-148) **HECATE.**
Yes, sir, all this is true. By chance,
Why do you stand as in a trance?
Come, sisters, let's lift his morale,
And show him what we can regale,
I'll charm the air to make a sound
While you perform your dance around,
So this great King can kindly say,
His duty we did on this day.

Music plays, the Witches and Hecate dance, then vanish, along with all their accoutrements. The cave is suddenly less threatening and appears to become a cellar, with barrels scattered about.

(141-148) ***HECATE.***
Ay, sir, all this is so:—but why
Stands Macbeth thus amazedly?—
Come, sisters, cheer we up his sprites,
And show the best of our delights.
I'll charm the air to give a sound,
While you perform your antic round;
That this great king may kindly say,
Our duties did his welcome pay.

Music. The Witches dance, and vanish.

(149-151) **MACBETH.**
Where are they? Gone? Then let this foul hour forever be flagged as evil…

Footsteps are heard outside.

Come in, whoever's near.

Lennox, passing nearby, enters through the open cellar door.

(149-151) ***MACBETH.***
Where are they? Gone?—Let this pernicious hour
Stand aye accursed in the calendar!—
Come in, without there!

Enter Lennox.

(151) **LENNOX.**
How can I help you, your highness?

(151) ***LENNOX.***
What's your Grace's will?

(152) **MACBETH.**
Did you see the witches?

(152) ***MACBETH.***
Saw you the Weird Sisters?

(152) **LENNOX.**
Witches? No, my lord.

(152) ***LENNOX.***
No, my lord.

(153) **MACBETH.**
Did they not go past you?

(153) ***MACBETH.***
Came they not by you?

(153) **LENNOX.**
No. I saw no witches, my lord.

(153) ***LENNOX.***
No, indeed, my lord.

(154-156) **MACBETH.**
Wherever they go, the air is polluted, and damned is anyone who trusts them. I heard the galloping of a horse. Who was it that rode past?

(154-156) ***MACBETH.***
Infected be the air whereon they ride;
And damn'd all those that trust them!—I did hear
The galloping of horse: who was't came by?

(157-158) **LENNOX.**
Oh, it was two or three messengers bringing news, my lord, that Macduff has fled to England.

(157-158) ***LENNOX.***

'Tis two or three, my lord, that bring you word
Macduff is fled to England.

(158) **MACBETH.**
Fled to England?

(158) ***MACBETH.***
Fled to England!

(159) **LENNOX.**
Yes, my good lord.

(159) ***LENNOX.***
Ay, my good lord.

(160-172) **MACBETH.** *To himself.*
Fleet-footed time has hindered my plans. My opportunity has passed. Of course, the time for action is lost if it is not seized immediately. From this time forth, as soon as my heart beckons me, my hands will respond accordingly.

And even at this very moment still, I can crown my plots with action. I think it, therefore it will be done. I will strike Macduff's castle, seize Fife and slice with my sword his wife, his children, and any other of his unfortunate relations I can find.

But no more boasting like a fool. I'll do this deed now, before my resolve cools. And no more phantoms!

Speaking to Lennox.
Where are these messengers? Come on, take me to where they are.

(160-172) ***MACBETH.***
Time, thou anticipat'st my dread exploits:
The flighty purpose never is o'ertook
Unless the deed go with it. From this moment
The very firstlings of my heart shall be
The firstlings of my hand. And even now,
To crown my thoughts with acts, be it thought and done:
The castle of Macduff I will surprise;
Seize upon Fife; give to th' edge o' th' sword
His wife, his babes, and all unfortunate souls
That trace him in his line. No boasting like a fool;
This deed I'll do before this purpose cool:
But no more sights!—Where are these gentlemen?

Come, bring me where they are.

Macbeth and Lennox exit the cellar.

ACT FOUR

SCENE TWO

In a room in Macduff's castle in Fife, Lady Macduff, seated, waits with her son, and Ross.

MODERN TRANSLATION:

ORIGINAL LANGUAGE:

(1) **LADY MACDUFF.**
But he's done nothing that requires him to flee.

(1) LADY MACDUFF.
What had he done, to make him fly the land?

(2) **ROSS.**
You must have patience, madam.

(2) ROSS.
You must have patience, madam.

(2-4) **LADY MACDUFF.**
He has no patience. It's complete madness. Though our conduct is blameless, his panic makes it look as though we're guilty of something.

(2-4) LADY MACDUFF.
He had none:
His flight was madness: when our actions do not,
Our fears do make us traitors.

(4-5) **ROSS.**
You don't know whether it was his panic, or rather his wisdom, that made him flee, madam.

(4-5) ROSS.
You know not
Whether it was his wisdom or his fear.

(6-14) **LADY MACDUFF.**
Wisdom? To leave his wife, his kids, his

mansion, his estate. To leave us all! And where does he leave us? Here, where he's not even willing to keep himself! He doesn't love us. He lacks even the most natural affections, obviously. Even a little wren, the smallest of birds, will fight an owl for the chicks in her nest. He is all fear and no love. I believe there is very little wisdom, when fleeing goes against all reason.

(6-14) ***LADY MACDUFF.***

Wisdom! to leave his wife, to leave his babes,
His mansion, and his titles, in a place
From whence himself does fly? He loves us not:
He wants the natural touch; for the poor wren,
The most diminutive of birds, will fight,
Her young ones in her nest, against the owl.
All is the fear, and nothing is the love;
As little is the wisdom, where the flight
So runs against all reason.

(14-26) **ROSS.**

My dear lady, please control yourself. For your husband's sake, if not yours. He is noble, wise, judicious and knows best what to do in the current climate. I dare not speak on this topic any further, but, oh, it is a very sad time indeed, when good people are denounced as traitors, when even they do not have a clue why.

We listen to rumours because we are paranoid, yet the rumours are so vague we are not sure why we are paranoid. These rumours float upon a wild and violent sea, and God knows where they will go or if they will sink or swim. I must make my farewell now, I'm afraid.

It won't be long until I return. And surely things cannot get any worse. They must soon climb to where they were once before. God bless you, my sweet cousin.

(14-26) ***ROSS.***

My dearest coz,
I pray you, school yourself: but, for your husband,
He is noble, wise, judicious, and best knows
The fits o' th' season. I dare not speak much further:
But cruel are the times, when we are traitors,

And do not know ourselves; when we hold rumour
From what we fear, yet know not what we fear,
But float upon a wild and violent sea
Each way and move—I take my leave of you:
Shall not be long but I'll be here again.
Things at the worst will cease, or else climb upward
To what they were before.—My pretty cousin,
Blessing upon you!

(27) **LADY MACDUFF.**
My son may technically have a father, but his father has abandoned him.

(27) LADY MACDUFF.
Father'd he is, and yet he's fatherless.

(28-30) **ROSS.**
Oh, my lady, it would be imprudent of me to stay a moment longer. For I'd only weep like a baby, and you'd only feel embarrassment at my weaknesses. I must leave at once.

Ross exits.

(28-30) ROSS.
I am so much a fool, should I stay longer,
It would be my disgrace and your discomfort:
I take my leave at once.

Exit.

(30-31) **LADY MACDUFF.**
My dear boy, your father is dead. And how will you survive? How will you live?

(30-31) LADY MACDUFF.
Sirrah, your father's dead.
And what will you do now? How will you live?

(32) **MACDUFF'S SON.**
As birds do, mama.

(32) MACDUFF'S SON.
As birds do, mother.

(32) **LADY MACDUFF.**
What, by eating worms and flies?

(32) LADY MACDUFF.
What, with worms and flies?

(33) **MACDUFF'S SON.**
No silly, I mean I will live by whatever comes my way, as they do.

(33) **MACDUFF'S SON.**

With what I get, I mean; and so do they.

(34-35) **LADY MACDUFF.**
My poor chick, you know not the nets and traps that may be set for you by huntsmen.

(34-35) LADY MACDUFF.
Poor bird! thou'dst never fear the net nor lime,
The pit-fall nor the gin.

(36-37) **MACDUFF'S SON.**
But why should I, mama? Silly birds don't know what hunters do. And anyway, my father's not dead, no matter what you say.

(36-37) MACDUFF'S SON.
Why should I, mother? Poor birds they are not set for.
My father is not dead, for all your saying.

(38) **LADY MACDUFF.**
Yes, he is dead. How will you do without a father?

(38) LADY MACDUFF.
Yes, he is dead: how wilt thou do for a father?

(39) **MACDUFF'S SON.**
No, rather how will you do without a husband?

(39) MACDUFF'S SON.
Nay, how will you do for a husband?

(40) **LADY MACDUFF.**
Oh, I could buy myself twenty new ones at any market.

(40) LADY MACDUFF.
Why, I can buy me twenty at any market.

(41) **MACDUFF'S SON.**
I bet you'd just buy them to sell them again at a profit.

(41) **MACDUFF'S SON.**
Then you'll buy 'em to sell again.

(42-43) **LADY MACDUFF.**
You speak with all your wit, son, and yet, by God, you do have wit in plenty.

(42-43) LADY MACDUFF.
Thou speak'st with all thy wit;
And yet, i' faith, with wit enough for thee.

(44) **MACDUFF'S SON.**
Was my father a traitor, mama?

(44) **MACDUFF'S SON.**
Was my father a traitor, mother?

(45) **LADY MACDUFF.**
Yes, that he was, son.

(45) LADY MACDUFF.
Ay, that he was.

(46) **MACDUFF'S SON.**
What is a traitor?

(46) MACDUFF'S SON.
What is a traitor?

(47) **LADY MACDUFF.**
Oh, one that makes a promise, and then breaks it, making them a liar.

(47) LADY MACDUFF.
Why, one that swears and lies.

(48) **MACDUFF'S SON.**
And is anyone who does that called a traitor?

(48) **MACDUFF'S SON.**
And be all traitors that do so?

(49-50) **LADY MACDUFF.**
Anyone who does that is a traitor, son, and must be hanged.

(49-50) LADY MACDUFF.
Every one that does so is a traitor, and must be hanged.

(51-52) **MACDUFF'S SON.**
And they must all liars be hanged?

(51-52) **MACDUFF'S SON.**
And must they all be hanged that swear and lie?

(53) **LADY MACDUFF.**
Every one of them.

(53) LADY MACDUFF.
Every one.

(54) **MACDUFF'S SON.**
Who hangs them?

(54) MACDUFF'S SON.
Who must hang them?

(55) **LADY MACDUFF.**
Oh, the honest men.

(55) LADY MACDUFF.
Why, the honest men.

(56-58) **MACDUFF'S SON.**
Then the liars are fools, for there are more liars than honest men, so they could easily round them up and hang them instead.

(56-58) **MACDUFF'S SON.**

Then the liars and swearers are fools: for there are liars and swearers enough to beat the honest men and hang up them.

(59-60) **LADY MACDUFF.**
You are a clever one, little monkey! But how will you do without a father?

(59-60) LADY MACDUFF.
Now, God help thee, poor monkey! But how wilt thou do for a father?

(61-63) **MACDUFF'S SON.**
If he really were dead, then you'd be weeping for him. But if he is dead and you're not weeping, then I trust I should have a new father soon enough.

(61-63) **MACDUFF'S SON.**
If he were dead, you'ld weep for him: if you would not, it were a good sign that I should quickly have a new father.

(64) **LADY MACDUFF.**
Cheeky boy, the things you say!

A Messenger enters.

(64) LADY MACDUFF.
Poor prattler, how thou talk'st!

Enter a Messenger.

(65-73) **A MESSENGER.**
God bless you, dear lady. You do not know me, though I am well aware of who you are. I dread that some danger is on its way here directly. If you will condescend to take a poor man's advice, please depart from here immediately. Go, go with your little children! I fear that I am alarming you with my brusque manner, but when I think of what they might do to you! The danger is already too near. God bless you. I dare not stay any longer.

The Messenger exits.

(65-73) A MESSENGER.
Bless you, fair dame! I am not to you known,
Though in your state of honour I am perfect.
I doubt some danger does approach you nearly:
If you will take a homely man's advice,
Be not found here; hence, with your little ones.

To fright you thus, methinks, I am too savage;
To do worse to you were fell cruelty,
Which is too nigh your person. Heaven preserve you!
I dare abide no longer.

Exit.

(73-79) **LADY MACDUFF.**
Where can I go? I have done no one any harm.

But now I remember, in this life, if you lie and cheat, then you are lauded and rewarded. On the other hand, if you do anything good, then the only reward is your ruin. Knowing this, then why, dear God, do I put up that pathetic defence that 'I have done no one any harm'.

A murderer enters.

Who are you?

(73-79) ***LADY MACDUFF.***
Whither should I fly?
I have done no harm. But I remember now
I am in this earthly world, where to do harm
Is often laudable; to do good sometime
Accounted dangerous folly: why then, alas,
Do I put up that womanly defence,
To say I have done no harm? What are these faces?

Enter Murderer.

(80) **A MURDERER.**
Where is your husband?

(80) A MURDERER.
Where is your husband?

(81-82) **LADY MACDUFF.**
I hope he's nowhere where someone like you would be allowed to enter.

(81-82) ***LADY MACDUFF.***
I hope, in no place so unsanctified
Where such as thou mayst find him.

(82) **A MURDERER.**
He is a traitor.

(82) **A MURDERER.**
He's a traitor.

(83) **MACDUFF'S SON.** *Attacking the Murderer.*
You liar, you hairy thug.

(83) MACDUFF'S SON.
Thou liest, thou shag-ear'd villain!

(83-84) **A MURDERER.** *Stabbing Macduff's son.*
What did you say, you spoiled brat! You traitor's calf!

(83-84) A MURDERER.
What, you egg!

Stabbing him.

Young fry of treachery!

(84-85) **MACDUFF'S SON.**
He has killed me, mama. Runaway, mama. Runaway!

Her son dies.

(84-85) MACDUFF'S SON.
He has kill'd me, mother:
Run away, I pray you!

(86) **LADY MACDUFF.**
Murderer!

(86) LADY MACDUFF.
Murderer!

She flees running from her room, chased by the Murderer, who leaves her son's dead body.

ACT FOUR

SCENE THREE

In England, in the gardens before the palace of the King of England, Edward. Malcolm and Macduff are having a discussion, alone.

MODERN TRANSLATION:

ORIGINAL LANGUAGE:

(1-2) **MALCOLM.**
Let's find some bleak shady spot, where we can weep until our wells run dry.

(1-2) ***MALCOLM.***
Let us seek out some desolate shade and there
Weep our sad bosoms empty.

(2-8) **MACDUFF.**
No, we must instead grasp our lethal swords, and like brave men, free our oppressed nation. Every new dawn, new widows mourn, new orphans cry, and new sorrows strike heaven flush in its face. Heaven screams out in agony, and in solidarity with Scotland's pain.

(2-8) ***MACDUFF.***
Let us rather
Hold fast the mortal sword, and, like good men,
Bestride our down-fall'n birthdom. Each new morn
New widows howl, new orphans cry; new sorrows
Strike heaven on the face, that it resounds
As if it felt with Scotland, and yell'd out
Like syllable of dolour.

(8-17) **MALCOLM.**
I'll scream at what offends me. I'll believe what I know. And I'll avenge when the time is right. What you have said, may turn out to be true.

That Mac… tyrant, the mere mention of whose name blisters my tongue, was once said to be an honest man.

And you were his good friend. And he has not injured you yet. And I am young, and you may find it prudent to betray me to him. Indeed, it is probably wise to offer up a weak poor innocent lamb in order to appease an angry god.

(8-17) ***MALCOLM.***
What I believe, I'll wail;
What know, believe; and what I can redress,
As I shall find the time to friend, I will.
What you have spoke, it may be so, perchance.
This tyrant, whose sole name blisters our tongues,
Was once thought honest: you have loved him well;
He hath not touch'd you yet. I am young; but something
You may deserve of him through me; and wisdom
To offer up a weak, poor, innocent lamb
To appease an angry god.

(18) **MACDUFF.**
I am not a traitor.

(18) ***MACDUFF.***
I am not treacherous.

(19-25) **MALCOLM.**
But Macbeth is. And a good and virtuous man may give in to a royal decree. But I still beg your pity. Your goodness and your virtue cannot be annulled. Angels are innocent, even though Satan fell. It is well known that evil people often wear a mask of virtue to disguise their cruelty, so how on earth can one be sure whether one's virtue is real or fake.

(19-25) ***MALCOLM.***
But Macbeth is.
A good and virtuous nature may recoil
In an imperial charge. But I shall crave your pardon.
That which you are, my thoughts cannot transpose.
Angels are bright still, though the brightest fell:
Though all things foul would wear the brows of grace,
Yet grace must still look so.

(25) **MACDUFF.**
I have lost all my hope.

(25) ***MACDUFF.***

I have lost my hopes.

(26-32) **MALCOLM.**
Perhaps you have lost your hope in the same place I found my doubts about you. Namely, why did you leave your wife and children in so defenceless a state?

Your dearest ones, those who you must be bound to with such sturdy knots of love. And yet you didn't even have the heart to say goodbye to them? I beg you, please do not let my suspicions become your fate. They are only for my own protection. You may well still be a good and honourable man, no matter my reservations.

(26-32) ***MALCOLM.***
Perchance even there where I did find my doubts.
Why in that rawness left you wife and child,
Those precious motives, those strong knots of love,
Without leave-taking?—I pray you,
Let not my jealousies be your dishonours,
But mine own safeties. You may be rightly just,
Whatever I shall think.

(32-38) **MACDUFF.**
You are damned, damned, wretched Scotland!

Tyranny, you can lay your foundations there safely, for there is no one worthy to thwart you. You can wear your false crown, Macbeth. The part of King is yours. Farewell, Malcolm. I swear that I would not be the villain you claim me to be, not for all the land in the tyrant's false hand, or all the riches in Asia.

(32-38) ***MACDUFF.***
Bleed, bleed, poor country!
Great tyranny, lay thou thy basis sure,
For goodness dare not check thee! wear thou thy wrongs;
The title is affeer'd.—Fare thee well, lord:
I would not be the villain that thou think'st
For the whole space that's in the tyrant's grasp
And the rich East to boot.

(38-50) **MALCOLM.**
Don't be offended. And please don't speak as though I distrust you entirely. Our country is sinking under the weight of tyranny. It weeps, it

bleeds, and each new day a new wound is cut. I believe, nonetheless, that there would be many that would support me, and the King of England himself has offered me an army of thousands.

But despite this, even if the tyrant's head was beneath my foot, or it was impaled on my sword, pitiful Scotland would be even more divided than ever before. And it would continue to suffer in ways presently unimaginable, under the hand of he that would succeed the tyrant.

(38-50) ***MALCOLM.***
Be not offended:
I speak not as in absolute fear of you.
I think our country sinks beneath the yoke;
It weeps, it bleeds; and each new day a gash
Is added to her wounds. I think, withal,
There would be hands uplifted in my right;
And here, from gracious England, have I offer
Of goodly thousands: but, for all this,
When I shall tread upon the tyrant's head,
Or wear it on my sword, yet my poor country
Shall have more vices than it had before,
More suffer, and more sundry ways than ever,
By him that shall succeed.

(50) **MACDUFF.**
And who would that be?

(50) ***MACDUFF.***
What should he be?

(51-56) **MALCOLM.**
I speak of myself. My vices, which I know in myself, will then be known to others, and these will make the shameless Macbeth seem as pure as the whitest snow. The poor public will then see him as not a tyrant, but as a lamb, when you compare him to my immeasurable faults.

(51-56) ***MALCOLM.***
It is myself I mean; in whom I know
All the particulars of vice so grafted
That, when they shall be open'd, black Macbeth
Will seem as pure as snow; and the poor state
Esteem him as a lamb, being compar'd
With my confineless harms.

(56-58) **MACDUFF.**
Not in all the armies of hell could there be an eviler devil to match the villainy of our Macbeth.

(56-58) MACDUFF.
Not in the legions
Of horrid hell can come a devil more damn'd
In evils to top Macbeth.

(58-67) **MALCOLM.**
I grant that he is violent, lewd, greedy, false, deceitful, angry and malicious. Any sin you can name, he can claim.

But, on my own part, to speak quite frankly, I am as horny as a goat. All your wives, your daughters, your matrons, your maids and your maidens could not quench my thirst for flesh. My uncontrollable desire would overwhelm any impediment in its way. I would seduce the innocent and nor would I suffer any rejection. Yes, better for Macbeth to rule, than a sexual predator such as I.

(58-67) MALCOLM.
I grant him bloody,
Luxurious, avaricious, false, deceitful,
Sudden, malicious, smacking of every sin
That has a name: but there's no bottom, none,
In my voluptuousness: your wives, your daughters,
Your matrons, and your maids, could not fill up
The cistern of my lust; and my desire
All continent impediments would o'erbear,
That did oppose my will: better Macbeth
Than such an one to reign.

(67-77) **MACDUFF.**
I grant that boundless lust can be a tyrannical power over a man. It has been known to be the downfall of many a worthy leader. But you should not let it stand in your way. Take what is rightfully yours! You can always satisfy your desires discreetly, and dress it in a cloak of purity for the public view.

The public can be easily deceived, and I can assure you that there would be no shortage of discreet women willing to satisfy your every need. Surely, sir, your desire cannot be so great that it cannot be satiated by the sheer mass of beautiful women that would consent to willingly gratify such a great man as you, if you were king.

(67-77) ***MACDUFF.***
Boundless intemperance
In nature is a tyranny; it hath been
Th' untimely emptying of the happy throne,
And fall of many kings. But fear not yet
To take upon you what is yours: you may
Convey your pleasures in a spacious plenty,
And yet seem cold—the time you may so hoodwink.
We have willing dames enough; there cannot be
That vulture in you, to devour so many
As will to greatness dedicate themselves,
Finding it so inclin'd.

(77-85) **MALCOLM.**
Yes, but it is not only that. In my soul, I fear I have an insatiable greed as well. And if I were king, then I would be unable to resist taking all the nobles' lands, I'd covet the jewels of one, and the house of another. And this would serve only as a taster. My hunger for luxuries would grow and grow, until I had started gratuitous disputes with all my good and loyal subjects. I'd have them destitute only for the benefit of feeding my own greed.

(77-85) ***MALCOLM.***
With this there grows
In my most ill-compos'd affection such
A staunchless avarice, that, were I king,
I should cut off the nobles for their lands;
Desire his jewels, and this other's house:
And my more-having would be as a sauce
To make me hunger more; that I should forge
Quarrels unjust against the good and loyal,
Destroying them for wealth.

(85-91) **MACDUFF.**
I fear your greed has deeper roots than the passing bloom of your lust. It has undone kings before, too. But do not worry about this either. Scotland's wealth is abundant, and it all springs from the royal palace that will be your own home. In any case, these imperfections are

enclosed in the overwhelming mass of your good traits.

(85-91) ***MACDUFF.***
This avarice
Sticks deeper; grows with more pernicious root
Than summer-seeming lust; and it hath been
The sword of our slain kings: yet do not fear;
Scotland hath foisons to fill up your will,
Of your mere own. All these are portable,
With other graces weigh'd.

(91-101) **MALCOLM.**
Good traits? I have none. The traits becoming to a king, such as justice, honesty, self-restraint, dependability, generosity, perseverance, mercy, humility, devotion, patience, courage, and determination, I have no trace of any of them.

I instead abound in their sinful opposites, and in each embody an astonishing deviation from the ideal. No, if I was given power, then I would only pour the sweet milk of harmony into the throats of hell, destroy all peace and undermine all unity on the face of the earth.

(91-101) ***MALCOLM.***
But I have none: the king-becoming graces,
As justice, verity, temp'rance, stableness,
Bounty, perseverance, mercy, lowliness,
Devotion, patience, courage, fortitude,
I have no relish of them; but abound
In the division of each several crime,
Acting it many ways. Nay, had I power, I should
Pour the sweet milk of concord into hell,
Uproar the universal peace, confound
All unity on earth.

(101) **MACDUFF.**
Oh, Scotland, poor Scotland!

(101) ***MACDUFF.***
O Scotland, Scotland!

(102-103) **MALCOLM.**
If anyone is fit to govern, then let them speak. For myself, I am as I have told.

(102-103) ***MALCOLM.***
If such a one be fit to govern, speak:
I am as I have spoken.

(103-115) **MACDUFF.**
Fit to govern? No, we're all unfit even to live. An illegitimate tyrant, with spots of blood still drying on the throne. Oh, our miserable nation, when will you see some good days again. And the truest heir, who is condemned by his own declaration of unworthiness, does desecrate what should be his to inherit.

Your royal father was a most saintly king. The Queen that gave you birth, was more often down on her knees praying than she was on her feet. She paid homage to God every day that she lived. I wish you well, sir. These sins that you confess mean that I can never return to Scotland.

Ah, my heart – all hope ends now!

*(103-115) **MACDUFF.***
Fit to govern?
No, not to live.—O nation miserable,
With an untitled tyrant bloody-scepter'd,
When shalt thou see thy wholesome days again,
Since that the truest issue of thy throne
By his own interdiction stands accus'd,
And does blaspheme his breed? Thy royal father
Was a most sainted king. The queen that bore thee,
Oft'ner upon her knees than on her feet,
Died every day she lived. Fare thee well!
These evils thou repeat'st upon thyself
Have banish'd me from Scotland.—O my breast,
Thy hope ends here!

(115-138) **MALCOLM.**
Macduff, your noble passion, a symbol of your integrity, has suddenly cleared the gloomy doubts from my soul.

Your words have stirred me to accept the truth of your goodness and honour. That devilish Macbeth has devised various strategies in order to win me over to his side, and my cautious restraint stops me from trusting anyone too quickly. But God above, may you reconcile us two, for I now wish to take your side, and I retract all the slander I may have just applied to you, and to my own self. I renounce all the faults and denunciations I pronounced, as fearful traitors passing over my own good character.

In actual fact, I have no real experience of women, I've not even seduced one. And I barely even care for my own possessions, let alone covet others. I have never deviated from my faith in God above, would not even betray the devil himself, and I value truthfulness as much as my life itself. The only lies I've ever spoken are those I've told against myself just now.

What I truly am is your, and my poor country's, servant. I am under the command of both. And, just before you arrived, Siward, the Earl of Northumberland, with ten thousand soldiers already prepared for battle, was about to head off for Scotland. Now, we can all go there as one. Let our chances of victory equal the justice of our fight!

(115-138) ***MALCOLM.***
Macduff, this noble passion,
Child of integrity, hath from my soul
Wiped the black scruples, reconcil'd my thoughts
To thy good truth and honour. Devilish Macbeth
By many of these trains hath sought to win me
Into his power, and modest wisdom plucks me
From over-credulous haste: but God above
Deal between thee and me! for even now
I put myself to thy direction, and
Unspeak mine own detraction; here abjure
The taints and blames I laid upon myself,
For strangers to my nature. I am yet
Unknown to woman; never was forsworn;
Scarcely have coveted what was mine own;
At no time broke my faith; would not betray
The devil to his fellow; and delight
No less in truth than life: my first false speaking
Was this upon myself. What I am truly,
Is thine and my poor country's to command:
Whither, indeed, before thy here-approach,
Old Siward, with ten thousand warlike men,
Already at a point, was setting forth.

Now we'll together, and the chance of goodness
Be like our warranted quarrel. Why are you silent?

(139-140) **MACDUFF.**
So many contradictory things said all at once. It is quite hard for one to comprehend.

An English Doctor arrives.

(139-140) MACDUFF.
Such welcome and unwelcome things at once
'Tis hard to reconcile.

Enter a Doctor.

(141) **MALCOLM.**
Well, we'll talk more about it shortly. Doctor, is the King of England on his way? Please tell me.

(141) MALCOLM.
Well; more anon.—Comes the King forth, I pray you?

(142-146) **ENGLISH DOCTOR.**
Yes, sir. There is a group of diseased souls that are awaiting his treatment. The best efforts of medical science are defeated by this illness, but the plain touch of the King heals them, such a holy power has heaven put in his hand.

(142-146) ENGLISH DOCTOR.
Ay, sir. There are a crew of wretched souls
That stay his cure: their malady convinces
The great assay of art; but at his touch,
Such sanctity hath heaven given his hand,
They presently amend.

(146) **MALCOLM.**
Thank you, doctor.

The English Doctor leaves.

(146) MALCOLM.
I thank you, doctor.

Exit Doctor.

(147) **MACDUFF.**
What is the illness he speaks of?

(147) MACDUFF.
What's the disease he means?

(147-160) **MALCOLM.**
It is tuberculosis – the 'King's evil', as it is called, as himself is the only cure. A most

miraculous thing indeed. I've witnessed him do it many times since I've been in England. How he attains heaven's help, God, and he, only know, but I've seen cruelly suffering patients, all swollen and ulcerous, most pitiful to see, who cannot be treated by any other means, cured by the king.

He simply hangs a golden coin, with holy prayers, around their neck. It is said that his children will also inherit this healing power. This rare gift also gives him the ability to prophecies. It is said he has a number of other divine gifts as well, all of which are surely a sign of his favour in the eyes of God.

Ross enters.

(147-160) ***MALCOLM.***
'Tis call'd the evil:
A most miraculous work in this good king;
Which often, since my here-remain in England,
I have seen him do. How he solicits heaven,
Himself best knows, but strangely-visited people,
All swoln and ulcerous, pitiful to the eye,
The mere despair of surgery, he cures;
Hanging a golden stamp about their necks,
Put on with holy prayers: and 'tis spoken,
To the succeeding royalty he leaves
The healing benediction. With this strange virtue,
He hath a heavenly gift of prophecy;
And sundry blessings hang about his throne,
That speak him full of grace.

Enter Ross.

(160) **MACDUFF.**
Look who's come.

(160) ***MACDUFF.***
See, who comes here?

(161) **MALCOLM.**
I see he's a fellow Scot, but I know him not.

(161) ***MALCOLM.***
My countryman; but yet I know him not.

(162) **MACDUFF.** *To Ross.*
My gentle cousin, welcome!

(162) ***MACDUFF.***
My ever-gentle cousin, welcome hither.

(163-164) **MALCOLM.**
Ah! Now I recognise him! Dear God, please end this chaos. We get to see our friends so seldomly that they begin to look like strangers to us!

(163-164) ***MALCOLM.***
I know him now. Good God, betimes remove
The means that makes us strangers!

(164) **ROSS.**
Amen to that, sir.

(164) ***ROSS.***
Sir, amen.

(165) **MACDUFF.**
Scotland remains in its perilous state?

(165) ***MACDUFF.***
Stands Scotland where it did?

(165-174) **ROSS.**
Sadly, our poor country is frightened of itself. It cannot be considered our home, but rather our grave, a place where only the ignorant are happy. A place where sighs and groans and screams fill the air, and all of these lamentations are considered unremarkable as they happen so frequently.

Yes, Scotland is a place where violent sorrow is commonplace. When bells ring for the dead, no one bothers to ask form whom it tolls, as the sound has grown familiar by its regularity. It's a place where ordinary men will die quicker than the flowers that they plucked that morning, as an adornment for their hat. The only perverse positive is that it's a place where few are sick, for most have already died of violent means before they get the chance.

(165-174) ***ROSS.***
Alas, poor country,
Almost afraid to know itself! It cannot
Be call'd our mother, but our grave, where nothing,
But who knows nothing, is once seen to smile;
Where sighs, and groans, and shrieks, that rent the air,
Are made, not mark'd; where violent sorrow seems

A modern ecstasy. The dead man's knell
Is there scarce ask'd for who; and good men's lives
Expire before the flowers in their caps,
Dying or ere they sicken.

(174-175) **MACDUFF.**
Oh, too well said, for it is all too true.

(174-175) ***MACDUFF.***
O, relation
Too nice, and yet too true!

(175) **MALCOLM.**
What is the latest misery to befall it.

(175) ***MALCOLM.***
What's the newest grief?

(176-177) **ROSS.**
News of an hour ago is already decried as old news. Every minute breeds a new misery.

(176-177) ***ROSS.***
That of an hour's age doth hiss the speaker;
Each minute teems a new one.

(177) **MACDUFF.**
How is my wife?

(177) ***MACDUFF.***
How does my wife?

(178) **ROSS.**
Um, she is well.

(178) ***ROSS.***
Why, well.

(178) **MACDUFF.**
And my children?

(178) ***MACDUFF.***
And all my children?

(178) **ROSS.**
Yes… they are well too.

(178) ***ROSS.***
Well too.

(179) **MACDUFF.**
Macbeth is not persecuting them?

(179) ***MACDUFF.***
The tyrant has not batter'd at their peace?

(180) **ROSS.**
No, all was well when I left them.

(180) ***ROSS.***
No; they were well at peace when I did leave 'em.

(181) **MACDUFF.**
Don't patronise me. Tell me what is happening there!

*(181) **MACDUFF.***
Be not a niggard of your speech: how goes't?

(182-189) **ROSS.**
When I left to bring you this solemn update, there was a rumour that there were many reputable men that were making for battle. This rumour was made credible by the fact that I saw Macbeth's army parading. We need help now.

Malcolm, if you returned to Scotland, it would surely help recruit soldiers for our cause, men and women both, as our cause is that just.

*(182-189) **ROSS.***
When I came hither to transport the tidings,
Which I have heavily borne, there ran a rumour
Of many worthy fellows that were out;
Which was to my belief witness'd the rather,
For that I saw the tyrant's power afoot.
Now is the time of help. Your eye in Scotland
Would create soldiers, make our women fight,
To doff their dire distresses.

(189-193) **MALCOLM.**
Whether they want it or not, we are coming home. The gracious King of England has given us Siward, the Earl of Northumberland, and his ten thousand soldiers. There is no more experienced, and no more commendable, soldier in any Christian country, than Siward is.

*(189-193) **MALCOLM.***
Be't their comfort
We are coming thither. Gracious England hath
Lent us good Siward and ten thousand men;
An older and a better soldier none
That Christendom gives out.

(193-196) **ROSS.**
I wish I could reply to this wonderful news with some of my own. But, unfortunately, the only intelligence I have to report is that which should only be screamed out in a vast desert where no one would be able to hear it. It is that bad.

*(193-196) **ROSS.***

Would I could answer
This comfort with the like! But I have words
That would be howl'd out in the desert air,
Where hearing should not latch them.

(196-198) **MACDUFF.**
What does this relate to? The generally perilous state of Scotland? Or is it something more personal. Something to tear the heart of only one of us?

(196-198) ***MACDUFF.***
What concern they?
The general cause? or is it a fee-grief
Due to some single breast?

(198-200) **ROSS.**
It would affect any right-thinking person, however, I must confess it touches you directly.

(198-200) ***ROSS.***
No mind that's honest
But in it shares some woe, though the main part
Pertains to you alone.

(200-201) **MACDUFF.**
Torture me no longer! If the news is mine, then tell me now!

(200-201) ***MACDUFF.***
If it be mine,
Keep it not from me, quickly let me have it.

(202-204) **ROSS.**
I only wish to ensure that your ears do not acquire an aversion to my tongue, as it is about to relate the worst thing they have ever heard.

(202-204) ***ROSS.***
Let not your ears despise my tongue for ever,
Which shall possess them with the heaviest sound
That ever yet they heard.

(204) **MACDUFF.**
I can guess at what it is.

(204) ***MACDUFF.***
Humh! I guess at it.

(205-208) **ROSS.**
Your castle was stormed, and your wife and children murdered. If I told you the manner of their death, it would surely kill you too.

(205-208) ***ROSS.***
Your castle is surpris'd; your wife and babes

Savagely slaughter'd. To relate the manner
Were, on the quarry of these murder'd deer,
To add the death of you.

(208-211) **MALCOLM.**
Heaven help us! Macduff, don't conceal your grief. Wear your heart on your sleeve. The grief that is not released, just builds up in your heart and bursts it.

(208-211) ***MALCOLM.***
Merciful heaven!—
What, man! ne'er pull your hat upon your brows.
Give sorrow words. The grief that does not speak
Whispers the o'er-fraught heart, and bids it break.

(212) **MACDUFF.**
My children too?

(212) ***MACDUFF.***
My children too?

(212-213) **ROSS.**
Wife, children, servants. All that could be found.

(212-213) ***ROSS.***
Wife, children, servants, all
That could be found.

(213-214) **MACDUFF.**
And I wasn't there to protect them! My wife was killed too?

(213-214) ***MACDUFF.***
And I must be from thence!
My wife kill'd too?

(214) **ROSS.**
I have told you, sir.

(214) ***ROSS.***
I have said.

(214-216) **MALCOLM.**
Please, be comforted. Our avenging army will be the medicine that cures your grief.

(214-216) ***MALCOLM.***
Be comforted:
Let's make us med'cines of our great revenge,
To cure this deadly grief.

(217-220) **MACDUFF.**
Macbeth has no children of his own. And he takes all my sweet children? Did you say all of them? Oh, hell bird! All? All my sweet and

innocent children taken in one fell swoop, like a hawk seizing its prey?

(217-220) ***MACDUFF.***
He has no children.—All my pretty ones?
Did you say all?—O hell-kite!—All?
What, all my pretty chickens and their dam
At one fell swoop?

(221) **MALCOLM.**
You must avenge them as a man possessed.

(221) ***MALCOLM.***
Dispute it like a man.

(222-229) **MACDUFF.**
And that I will. But I must also feel the pain like a man possessed. How can I not dwell on those who were most precious to me? Was heaven a witness to this horror and yet not lift a finger to help? Were they allowed to be slain because I was not pious enough? Yes, it is true, I am sinful. They were not killed for their own faults, but mine. I am the cause of their slaughter. May they rest in peace.

(222-229) ***MACDUFF.***
I shall do so;
But I must also feel it as a man:
I cannot but remember such things were,
That were most precious to me.—Did heaven look on,
And would not take their part? Sinful Macduff,
They were all struck for thee! Naught that I am,
Not for their own demerits, but for mine,
Fell slaughter on their souls: heaven rest them now!

(230-231) **MALCOLM.**
Let this sharpen your will to fight. Let your grief become anger. Don't console your heart, enrage it!

(230-231) ***MALCOLM.***
Be this the whetstone of your sword. Let grief
Convert to anger; blunt not the heart, enrage it.

(232-237) **MACDUFF.**
Oh, I am crying like a girl, but I can still be bold and boast of revenge with my tongue! Heavens above we can delay no longer. Bring this fiend who claims to be King of Scotland to my face, within the length of my sword, and he will

suffer my revenge. If he escapes, well heaven help him.

(232-237) ***MACDUFF.***
O, I could play the woman with mine eyes,
And braggart with my tongue!—But, gentle heavens,
Cut short all intermission; front to front,
Bring thou this fiend of Scotland and myself;
Within my sword's length set him; if he 'scape,
Heaven forgive him too!

(237-242) **MALCOLM.**
That's more like it. Manly words. Come, our army is ready. We must say farewell to the King of England, then, on to Scotland. Macbeth is ripe for the taking. Let heaven be our guide and protector. Do what you must to stoke your courage.

The night may be too long for some,
But day will surely always come.

(237-242) ***MALCOLM.***
This tune goes manly.
Come, go we to the King. Our power is ready;
Our lack is nothing but our leave. Macbeth
Is ripe for shaking, and the powers above
Put on their instruments. Receive what cheer you may;
The night is long that never finds the day.

They all depart to take their leave of King Edward of England and prepare to join Seward and his ten-thousand strong army on their quest to liberate Scotland from the tyrant Macbeth.

ACT FIVE

SCENE ONE

Macbeth, and his entourage, have moved to a castle in Dunsinane, where he considers himself safe. In a room within that castle, a Scottish Doctor enters, with Lady Macbeth's maid.

MODERN TRANSLATION:

ORIGINAL LANGUAGE:

(1-2) **SCOTTISH DOCTOR.**
I have been with you, observing, for two nights now. But I can't see any truth in what you claim. When did she last do it?

(1-2) ***SCOTTISH DOCTOR.***
I have two nights watched with you, but can perceive no truth in your report. When was it she last walked?

(3-7) **HER MAID.**
Well, since his majesty, Macbeth, went into battle, I have seen her rise from her bed, put on her nightgown, unlock her cabinet, take some paper out, and then fold it, write on it, read what she's written, then fold it up, and seal it shut tight, and then she returns to her bed.

(3-7) ***HER MAID.***
Since his Majesty went into the field, I have seen her rise from her bed, throw her nightgown upon her, unlock her closet, take forth paper, fold it, write upon't, read it, afterwards seal it, and again return to bed; yet all this while in a most fast sleep.

(8-11) **SCOTTISH DOCTOR.**
Hmm, a great distress must be affecting the subconscious, if she is both asleep and yet

active, and moving about. Sleepwalking we doctors term it. Whilst she is 'sleepwalking', aside from her walking and her actions, have you ever heard her actually say anything?

(8-11) ***SCOTTISH DOCTOR.***
A great perturbation in nature, to receive at once the benefit of sleep, and do the effects of watching. In this slumbery agitation, besides her walking and other actual performances, what, at any time,have you heard her say?

(12) **HER MAID.**
She has said things, sir, things which I can't repeat.

(12) ***HER MAID.***
That, sir, which I will not report after her.

(13) **SCOTTISH DOCTOR.**
Now, you may repeat them to me, dear. Indeed, it is only right that you should.

(13) ***SCOTTISH DOCTOR.***
You may to me; and 'tis most meet you should.

(14-17) **HER MAID.**
Not to you, and not to anyone, sir. Besides, no one else was with me to ensure I heard it all correctly.

Lady Macbeth enters.

Oh look, here she comes. This is precisely what she always does, I swear it on my husband's grave. Look at her, she is fast asleep, yet walking. Watch her! She can't see us.

(14-17) ***HER MAID.***
Neither to you nor anyone; having no witness to confirm my speech.

Enter Lady Macbeth with a torch.

Lo you, here she comes! This is her very guise; and, upon my life, fast asleep. Observe her; stand close.

(18) **SCOTTISH DOCTOR.**
Where did she get that lantern?

(18) ***SCOTTISH DOCTOR.***
How came she by that light?

(19-20) **HER MAID.**
It's always beside her bed. She has a lantern with

her always. She orders us to always have it there. She's very insistent about it.

(19-20) ***HER MAID.***
Why, it stood by her: she has light by her continually; 'tis her command.

(21) **SCOTTISH DOCTOR.**
You can see that her eyes are open.

(21) ***SCOTTISH DOCTOR.***
You see, her eyes are open.

(22) **HER MAID.**
Yes, but she can't see anything.

(22) ***HER MAID.***
Ay, but their sense are shut.

(23) **SCOTTISH DOCTOR.**
What is she doing now? Look at how she rubs her hands together.

(23) ***SCOTTISH DOCTOR.***
What is it she does now? Look how she rubs her hands.

(24-26) **HER MAID.**
Oh, she is always doing that. It's as if she is washing her hands. I have seen her doing just that alone for, say, fifteen minutes.

(24-26) ***HER MAID.***
It is an accustomed action with her, to seem thus washing her hands. I have known her to continue in this a quarter of an hour.

(27) **LADY MACBETH.**
Here's another spot.

(27) ***LADY MACBETH.***
Yet here's a spot.

(28-29) **SCOTTISH DOCTOR.**
Listen. She is speaking. I will write down what she says so we have it on record.

(28-29) ***SCOTTISH DOCTOR.***
Hark, she speaks. I will set down what comes from her, to satisfy my remembrance the more strongly.

(30-34) **LADY MACBETH.**
Off spot, evil spot, off. I tell you, off! One, two…

Why, then it is time to do what must be done. Hell is murky.

What, Macbeth, what, a soldier and afraid? We don't need to fear anyone knowing. What can they do, what can they do to my King Macbeth?

But who would've thought that the old man would've had so much blood in him?

(30-34) ***LADY MACBETH.***
Out, damned spot! out, I say! One; two. Why, then 'tis time to do't. Hell is murky! Fie, my lord, fie! a soldier, and afeard? What need we fear who knows it, when none can call our power to account? Yet who would have thought the old man to have had so much blood in him?

(35) **SCOTTISH DOCTOR.**
Did you hear that?

(35) ***SCOTTISH DOCTOR.***
Do you mark that?

(36-38) **LADY MACBETH.**
The Lord of Fife had a wife. Where is she now? Will these hands never be clean?

No more of that, Macbeth, no more of that. You'll ruin everything with your fussing about.

(36-38) ***LADY MACBETH.***
The Thane of Fife had a wife. Where is she now?— What, will these hands ne'er be clean? No more o' that, my lord, no more o' that: you mar all with this starting.

(39) **SCOTTISH DOCTOR.**
For shame, for shame. You've heard things you shouldn't.

(39) ***SCOTTISH DOCTOR.***
Go to, go to. You have known what you should not.

(40-41) **HER MAID.**
She's the one who's spoken things she shouldn't. I'm certain of that, sir. Whether she's also done things she shouldn't, well, God only knows.

(40-41) ***HER MAID.***
She has spoke what she should not, I am sure of that: heaven knows what she has known.

(42-43) **LADY MACBETH.**
I can still smell the blood. All the perfume in all the world can't sweeten the smell of these hands. Ah, ah, ah!

(42-43) ***LADY MACBETH.***

Here's the smell of the blood still: all the perfumes of Arabia will not sweeten this little hand. Oh, oh, oh!

(44) **SCOTTISH DOCTOR.**
What a sigh! Her heart is very heavily burdened.

(44) SCOTTISH DOCTOR.
What a sigh is there! The heart is sorely charged.

(45-46) **HER MAID.**
I wouldn't have that heart for anything, sir, not even if it meant I could be queen of all the world.

(45-46) HER MAID.
I would not have such a heart in my bosom for the dignity of the whole body.

(47) **SCOTTISH DOCTOR.**
Well, well, well.

(47) SCOTTISH DOCTOR.
Well, well, well.

(48) **HER MAID.**
I think only God could make her well again, sir.

(48) HER MAID.
Pray God it be, sir.

(49-51) **SCOTTISH DOCTOR.**
Her illness is beyond my knowledge. However, I have had many patients who sleepwalked for years, and still died respectably in their beds, like normal people.

(49-51) SCOTTISH DOCTOR.
This disease is beyond my practice: yet I have known those which have walked in their sleep, who have died holily in their beds.

(52-54) **LADY MACBETH.**
Wash your hands, put on your nightgown, don't look so pale. I tell you again, Banquo is buried. He can't rise out of his grave.

(52-54) LADY MACBETH.
Wash your hands, put on your nightgown; look not so pale. I tell you yet again, Banquo's buried; he cannot come out of his grave.

(55) **SCOTTISH DOCTOR.**
Can it be true?

(55) SCOTTISH DOCTOR.
Even so?

(56-58) **LADY MACBETH.**
To bed, to bed. There's knocking at the door.

Come, come, come, come, give me your hand. What's done cannot be undone.

To bed, to bed, to bed…

Lady Macbeth returns to her bedroom.

(56-58) ***LADY MACBETH.***
To bed, to bed. There's knocking at the gate. Come, come, come, come, give me your hand. What's done cannot be undone. To bed, to bed, to bed.

Exit.

(59) **SCOTTISH DOCTOR.**
Will she go back to bed now?

(59) ***SCOTTISH DOCTOR.***
Will she go now to bed?

(60) **HER MAID.**
That she will, sir.

(60) ***HER MAID.***
Directly.

(61-69) **SCOTTISH DOCTOR.**
Foul rumours are spreading. Evil deeds breed evil troubles. And troubled minds whisper to their unconscious pillows their secret thoughts. She needs a priest more than she needs me. God, please God, forgive us all!

You look after her as best you can. Remove anything that she may be able to harm herself with. But you must keep watching her.

I will go now. She has baffled my mind and amazed my sight. I will think about what she's said, but I dare not speak of it.

(61-69) ***SCOTTISH DOCTOR.***
Foul whisp'rings are abroad. Unnatural deeds
Do breed unnatural troubles: infected minds
To their deaf pillows will discharge their secrets.
More needs she the divine than the physician.—
God, God, forgive us all! Look after her;
Remove from her the means of all annoyance,
And still keep eyes upon her. So, good night:
My mind she has mated, and amaz'd my sight.
I think, but dare not speak.

(69) **HER MAID.**
Good night, good doctor.

(69) ***HER MAID.***
Good night, good doctor.

The Doctor and Lady Macbeth's maid leave the room

ACT FIVE

SCENE TWO

In the countryside near Dunsinane, Menteith, Caithness, Angus, Lennox and soldiers, with drummers and flags flying, gather.

MODERN TRANSLATION:

ORIGINAL LANGUAGE:

(1-5) **MENTEITH.**
The English army is near, led on by Malcolm, his uncle Siward, and Macduff. The fire of revenge burns in them all. But for their just cause, that fire could burn even in the dead buried in their graves, and rouse them to fight against the tyrant.

(1-5) ***MENTEITH.***
The English power is near, led on by Malcolm,
His uncle Siward, and the good Macduff.
Revenges burn in them; for their dear causes
Would to the bleeding and the grim alarm
Excite the mortified man.

(5-6) **ANGUS.**
We'll meet them near Birnam Wood. They are heading that way.

(5-6) ***ANGUS.***
Near Birnam wood
Shall we well meet them. That way are they coming.

(7) **CAITHNESS.**
Does anyone know if Donalbain is with his brother?

(7) ***CAITHNESS.***
Who knows if Donalbain be with his brother?

(8-11) **LENNOX.**
I am certain he is not, sir. I have a list of all the

nobility in action, and he is not on it. Young Siward's son is, though. And there are many other young men, still unbearded, who make their first claims to manhood.

(8-11) ***LENNOX.***
For certain, sir, he is not. I have a file
Of all the gentry: there is Siward's son
And many unrough youths, that even now
Protest their first of manhood.

(11) **MENTEITH.**
What is Macbeth doing?

(11) ***MENTEITH.***
What does the tyrant?

(12-16) **CAITHNESS.**
He is barricading at his castle at Dunsinane. Some of his men say he is completely crazy. Others more sympathetic, just call it 'heroic rage'. But this is certain: he can neither restrain his temper, nor justify his corrupt cause.

(12-16) ***CAITHNESS.***
Great Dunsinane he strongly fortifies.
Some say he's mad; others, that lesser hate him,
Do call it valiant fury: but, for certain,
He cannot buckle his distemper'd cause
Within the belt of rule.

(16-22) **ANGUS.**
I wonder if he finds that the guilt from his secret murders sticks in his mind just like the blood of Duncan stuck to his hands?

Every minute our armies are avenging his violations to order and justice with great passion and determination, whereas his army moves forward unwillingly, mechanically, and only by command, not by respect or love.

We fight for a 'just cause', they fight 'just because'. I bet he now finds the title of king unfitting, like a giant's cloak hanging limply upon a dwarfish thief.

(16-22) ***ANGUS.***
Now does he feel
His secret murders sticking on his hands;
Now minutely revolts upbraid his faith-breach;

Those he commands move only in command,
Nothing in love: now does he feel his title
Hang loose about him, like a giant's robe
Upon a dwarfish thief.

(22-25) **MENTEITH.**

Who could blame his tormented mind if it tried to break free from his body. All the organs lodged there must covet the same rebellion and denounce their tyrannical vessel.

(22-25) MENTEITH.

Who, then, shall blame
His pester'd senses to recoil and start,
When all that is within him does condemn
Itself for being there?

(25-29) **CAITHNESS.**

Men, we must march on in obedience to the just cause and meet with Malcolm, the only remedy for the diseased state of Scotland. We must pour all of ourselves into this medicine that will purge Macbeth from this land.

(25-29) CAITHNESS.

Well, march we on,
To give obedience where 'tis truly ow'd:
Meet we the med'cine of the sickly weal;
And with him pour we, in our country's purge,
Each drop of us.

(29-31) **LENNOX.**

Or at least enough of ourselves so that the royal flower can be sprinkled, and the usurping weed drowned. Let us march on towards Birnam.

(29-31) LENNOX.

Or so much as it needs
To dew the sovereign flower, and drown the weeds.
Make we our march towards Birnam.

The army marches on towards Birnam Wood.

ACT FIVE

SCENE THREE

At Dunsinane, in a room within the castle, Macbeth meets with his attendants and the Scottish Doctor.

MODERN TRANSLATION:

(1-12) **MACBETH.**
Bring me no more reports. Let all the lords abandon me, I don't care. I need not fear anything until Birnam Wood moves to Dunsinane Hill. What about that boy Malcolm? Was he not of a woman born? The witches that know the destinies of all men proclaimed this: 'Fear not, Macbeth. No man that is born of a woman will ever have any power over you.' So flee, you false lords, and mingle with those English dandies.

This mind I control and this heart I bear,
Will never sag with doubt, nor shake with fear.

A Servant enters.

The devil damn you to Hades, you pale-faced fool. What's with your face, you silly goose.

ORIGINAL LANGUAGE:

(1-12) ***MACBETH.***
Bring me no more reports; let them fly all:
Till Birnam wood remove to Dunsinane
I cannot taint with fear. What's the boy Malcolm?
Was he not born of woman? The spirits that know
All mortal consequences have pronounc'd me thus:
"Fear not, Macbeth; no man that's born of woman

Shall e'er have power upon thee."—Then fly, false thanes,
And mingle with the English epicures:
The mind I sway by, and the heart I bear,
Shall never sag with doubt nor shake with fear.

Enter a Servant.

The devil damn thee black, thou cream-fac'd loon!
Where gott'st thou that goose look?

(13) **A SERVANT.**
There are ten thousand…

(13) A SERVANT.
There is ten thousand—

(14) **MACBETH.**
Geese, coward?

(14) MACBETH.
Geese, villain?

(14) **A SERVANT.**
Soldiers, sir.

(14) A SERVANT.
Soldiers, sir.

(15-18) **MACBETH.**
Go slap some rouge on your face to hide your fear, you lily-livered boy! What soldiers, you twit?

Go to hell! Those cotton cheeks of yours will make the others as cowardly as you are!

What soldiers are you talking about, milky face?

(15-18) MACBETH.
Go prick thy face and over-red thy fear,
Thou lily-liver'd boy. What soldiers, patch?
Death of thy soul! those linen cheeks of thine
Are counsellors to fear. What soldiers, whey-face?

(19) **A SERVANT.**
The English army, if it please you or not, sir.

(19) A SERVANT.
The English force, so please you.

(20-30) **MACBETH.**
Remove your face from mine!

The Servant exits.

Seyton! – It sickens my heart when I see – Seyton! For Christ's sake! – This crisis will cheer me forever or it will dethrone me. But I have lived long enough. I'm in my autumn years. And I won't be allowed to have what should accompany old age anyway, such as honour, love, obedience, crowds of friends. No, I'll only be paid lip service to my face and have quiet curses, though they'll cut deep, traded behind my back. And beyond that, I only have my breath, which my heart would be happy to forsake, but I dare not.

Seyton!

Seyton enters.

(20-30) ***MACBETH.***
Take thy face hence.

Exit Servant.

Seyton!—I am sick at heart,
When I behold—Seyton, I say!—This push
Will cheer me ever or disseat me now.
I have liv'd long enough: my way of life
Is fall'n into the sere, the yellow leaf;
And that which should accompany old age,
As honour, love, obedience, troops of friends,
I must not look to have; but, in their stead,
Curses, not loud but deep, mouth-honour, breath,
Which the poor heart would fain deny, and dare not.
Seyton!—

Enter Seyton.

(31) **SEYTON.**
How can I help, sir?

(31) ***SEYTON.***
What's your gracious pleasure?

(31) **MACBETH.**
Do you have any more news?

(31) ***MACBETH.***
What news more?

(32) **SEYTON.**
I can only confirm what I reported earlier, sir.

(32) ***SEYTON.***
All is confirm'd, my lord, which was reported.

(33-34) **MACBETH.**
I'll keep on fighting till my flesh is hacked from my bones. Bring me my armour.

(33-34) ***MACBETH.***
I'll fight till from my bones my flesh be hack'd.
Give me my armour.

(35) **SEYTON.**
My lord, you don't need it yet.

(35) ***SEYTON.***
'Tis not needed yet.

(36-39) **MACBETH.**
I'll put it on anyway. Send out more horses to charge. Scour our fields and hang any who talk of fear…

And bring me my armour!

To the Scottish Doctor
How is my wife, doctor?

(36-39) ***MACBETH.***
I'll put it on.
Send out more horses, skirr the country round;
Hang those that talk of fear. Give me mine armour.—
How does your patient, doctor?

(39-41) **SCOTTISH DOCTOR.**
Not so much sick, my lord, as troubled in her mind by stubborn fantasies that prevent her from getting a good night's rest.

(39-41) **SCOTTISH DOCTOR.**
Not so sick, my lord,
As she is troubled with thick-coming fancies,
That keep her from her rest.

(41-47) **MACBETH.**
Then cure her of it!

Do you not know how to treat a diseased mind? Simply pull from their memory the rooted sorrow and scorch the worries engraved in their brain. And with some sweet potion of amnesia, cleanse the distraught chest of that hazardous mixture which weighs upon her heart.

(41-47) ***MACBETH.***
Cure her of that:
Canst thou not minister to a mind diseas'd,
Pluck from the memory a rooted sorrow,
Raze out the written troubles of the brain,
And with some sweet oblivious antidote
Cleanse the stuff'd bosom of that perilous stuff
Which weighs upon the heart?

(47-48) **SCOTTISH DOCTOR.**
In that scenario, the only means of treatment is within the patient themselves.

(47-48) ***SCOTTISH DOCTOR.***
Therein the patient
Must minister to himself.

(49-57) **MACBETH.**
Medicine is for dogs. I'll have none of it.

To an attendant.
Come here, help me to put on my armour. And give me my spear.

Seyton, send for my men.

Seyton exits.

Doctor, the lords leave me…

To the attendant.
Come here now, hurry!

To the Doctor.
If you could examine the urine of Scotland, to find what diseases her, and purge it from her, until she regains her good and pristine health. If you could do that, doctor, I would applaud you until it echoes, and echoes, and echoes ever more.

To the attendant.
Pull that off, I tell you! You idiot! It doesn't fit!

To the Doctor.

Would rhubarb, or herbs, or any drug, be able to purge the English from here? Have you heard that they are coming?

(49-57) ***MACBETH.***
Throw physic to the dogs, I'll none of it.
Come, put mine armour on; give me my staff:
Seyton, send out.—Doctor, the Thanes fly from me.—
Come, sir, despatch.—If thou couldst, doctor, cast
The water of my land, find her disease,
And purge it to a sound and pristine health,
I would applaud thee to the very echo,
That should applaud again.—Pull't off, I say.—
What rhubarb, senna, or what purgative drug,
Would scour these English hence? Hear'st thou of them?

(58-59) **SCOTTISH DOCTOR.**
Yes, my good lord. All the fear of war means news is spreading fast.

(58-59) ***SCOTTISH DOCTOR.***
Ay, my good lord. Your royal preparation
Makes us hear something.

(60-62) **MACBETH.** *To the attendant.*
Leave it! I'll put the rest of the armour on there.

Departing the room with his attendant.
I fear no death or destruction till,
Birnam Wood moves to Dunsinane Hill.

(60-62) ***MACBETH.***
Bring it after me.—
I will not be afraid of death and bane,
Till Birnam forest come to Dunsinane.

Exeunt all except Doctor.

(63-64) **SCOTTISH DOCTOR.** *To himself.*
Were I from Dunsinane I'd flee immediately,
I'd not return there for any large reward or fee.

(63-64) ***SCOTTISH DOCTOR.***
Were I from Dunsinane away and clear,
Profit again should hardly draw me here.

The Scottish Doctor exits.

ACT FIVE

SCENE FOUR

In the countryside near Dunsinane, with Birnam Wood within view, Malcolm, Siward, Macduff, young Siward, Menteith, Caithness, Angus and soldiers enter marching, with drummers, and flags flying.

MODERN TRANSLATION:

(1-2) **MALCOLM.**
My cousins, I hope that the day is near when all bedrooms in the country will be safe again.

(2) **MENTEITH.**
We don't doubt that day will come soon.

(3) **SIWARD.**
What forest is this here?

(3) **MENTEITH.**
Birnam Wood.

(4-7) **MALCOLM.**
Tell each soldier to cut down a branch and to hold it in front of him while he walks. It will act as camouflage and make the tyrant's spies report that our army is smaller than it actually is.

ORIGINAL LANGUAGE:

(1-2) ***MALCOLM.***
Cousins, I hope the days are near at hand
That chambers will be safe.

(2) ***MENTEITH.***
We doubt it nothing.

(3) ***SIWARD.***
What wood is this before us?

(3) ***MENTEITH.***
The wood of Birnam.

(4-7) ***MALCOLM.***

Let every soldier hew him down a bough,
And bear't before him. Thereby shall we shadow
The numbers of our host, and make discovery
Err in report of us.

(7) **A SOLDIER.**
I will tell them, sir.

The Soldier exits.

(7) A SOLDIER.
It shall be done.

(8-10) **SIWARD.**
We hear that the tyrant rests at his castle in Dunsinane, and that he is even happy to remain there whilst we lay siege to it.

(8-10) SIWARD.
We learn no other but the confident tyrant
Keeps still in Dunsinane, and will endure
Our setting down before't.

(10-14) **MALCOLM.**
It is his only hope. For where there has been any opportunity for his men, both high and low, they have taken it, and fled and deserted him.

The only ones left to fight for him are those who have been unable to flee. And for them, though their bodies may remain, their hearts have already left.

(10-14) MALCOLM.
'Tis his main hope;
For where there is advantage to be given,
Both more and less have given him the revolt,
And none serve with him but constrained things,
Whose hearts are absent too.

(14-16) **MACDUFF.**
This is mere talk, we can only know its veracity after the fact. We must fight on as though our lives depend on it.

(14-16) MACDUFF.
Let our just censures
Attend the true event, and put we on
Industrious soldiership.

(16-21) **SIWARD.**
Yes, that time is approaching, friends, where we will find out what is fiction and what is fact.

Our hopes direct our speculations. Only the battle itself can decide the outcome.

(16-21) ***SIWARD.***
The time approaches,
That will with due decision make us know
What we shall say we have, and what we owe.
Thoughts speculative their unsure hopes relate,
But certain issue strokes must arbitrate;
Towards which advance the war.

The army continues to march on towards Dunsinane, camouflaged by branches from Birnam Wood.

ACT FIVE

SCENE FIVE

At Dunsinane, within the castle grounds, Macbeth and Seyton, with fewer soldiers, enter with a drummer and their flags flying.

MODERN TRANSLATION:

(1-7) **MACBETH.**
Raise our flags on the outer walls. The news is still that 'they come'. But with the strength of our castle, their siege is laughable. Then let them lie here until they are eaten by starvation and malaria. And were their army not reinforced with 'my' treacherous soldiers, then we could have fought them brazenly, man to man, and beat them severely as they retreated home.

There is the sound of women crying from within the castle

What is that noise?

ORIGINAL LANGUAGE:

(1-7) ***MACBETH.***
Hang out our banners on the outward walls;
The cry is still, "They come!" Our castle's strength
Will laugh a siege to scorn: here let them lie
Till famine and the ague eat them up.
Were they not forc'd with those that should be ours,
We might have met them dareful, beard to beard,
And beat them backward home.

A cry of women within.

What is that noise?

(8) **SEYTON.**
It is the wailing of women, my lord.

Seyton exits.

(8) SEYTON.
It is the cry of women, my good lord.

Exit.

(9-15) **MACBETH.**
I had almost forgotten what fear is. Once upon a time, my senses too would've been chilled by dread, and to hear screams and sordid tales at night, well, it would've made the hair on my neck stand on end, as if it were alive. I have dined on horrors and had my fill. I am so accustomed to terror that it cannot shock me anymore.

Seyton re-enters.

What was that wailing for?

(9-15) MACBETH.
I have almost forgot the taste of fears.
The time has been, my senses would have cool'd
To hear a night-shriek; and my fell of hair
Would at a dismal treatise rouse and stir
As life were in't. I have supp'd full with horrors;
Direness, familiar to my slaughterous thoughts,
Cannot once start me.

Enter Seyton.

Wherefore was that cry?

(16) **SEYTON.**
Your Queen, my lord, is dead.

(16) SEYTON.
The Queen, my lord, is dead.

(16-28) **MACBETH.**
She should've waited. Maybe there'll be peace tomorrow.

'Peace tomorrow'. Ha! There was once a time for such words. Tomorrow, and tomorrow, and tomorrow again. Time creeps at a snail's pace from day to day. And one day, time'll reach its final scene, its final act. And all the yesterdays that have passed, what have they achieved? Nothing. Merely to send fools on their way to their deaths in the dust.

Extinguished, all extinguished, like a snuffed candle. Life's nothing but a shadow walking. A bad actor swaggering and fussing about, for their allotted hour on the stage of life. And then it's easily quenched, and they're gone. As if they had never even existed.

Ha! Life is a tale. Told by an idiot. Oh yes, we fill it all with all the sound and fury that we can. But, in the end, it all means, and was, nothing.

A Messenger enters.

You've come to speak to me I assume. Say it quickly.

(16-28) ***MACBETH.***
She should have died hereafter.
There would have been a time for such a word.
Tomorrow, and tomorrow, and tomorrow,
Creeps in this petty pace from day to day,
To the last syllable of recorded time;
And all our yesterdays have lighted fools
The way to dusty death. Out, out, brief candle!
Life's but a walking shadow; a poor player,
That struts and frets his hour upon the stage,
And then is heard no more: it is a tale
Told by an idiot, full of sound and fury,
Signifying nothing.

Enter a Messenger.

Thou com'st to use thy tongue; thy story quickly.

(28-30) **A MESSENGER.**
Your majesty, I, I should tell just you what I saw, but I, I, um, I don't know how to say it exactly.

(28-30) ***A MESSENGER.***
Gracious my lord,
I should report that which I say I saw,

But know not how to do't.

(30) **MACBETH.**
Come on, spit it out.

(30) MACBETH.
Well, say, sir.

(31-33) **A MESSENGER.**
As I, I was posted to watch Dunsinane Hill, I looked towards Birnam, and, and, then, then I thought I saw a forest moving.

(31-33) A MESSENGER.
As I did stand my watch upon the hill,
I look'd toward Birnam, and anon, methought,
The wood began to move.

(33) **MACBETH.**
Liar and imbecile!

(33) MACBETH.
Liar, and slave!

(34-36) **A MESSENGER.**
I would justly deserve your anger, sir, if I was not speaking the truth. But within three miles of Dunsinane Hill you can see it coming, sir, a moving forest.

(34-36) A MESSENGER.
Let me endure your wrath, if't be not so.
Within this three mile may you see it coming;
I say, a moving grove.

(36-50) **MACBETH.**
If you are lying to me, you will hang, alive, on this tree, until you starve to your death. And if you are telling me the truth, then you can hang me the same.

My resolve is failing me!

Those witches! They equivocate like the devil. They told lies like truths. 'Fear not until Birnam Wood, comes to Dunsinane'. And a forest is now ascending Dunsinane Hill.

Arm yourself, arm yourself, arm yourself for battle!

If what he says is true, then there is no use fleeing or hiding…

I begin to grow weary of the sun.
And wish the world could be snuffed and undone
Ring the alarms. Tempests all destroy.
We'll die fighting; our armour let's employ.

(36-50) ***MACBETH.***

If thou speak'st false,
Upon the next tree shalt thou hang alive,
Till famine cling thee: if thy speech be sooth,
I care not if thou dost for me as much.—
I pull in resolution; and begin
To doubt th' equivocation of the fiend,
That lies like truth. "Fear not, till Birnam wood
Do come to Dunsinane;" and now a wood
Comes toward Dunsinane.—Arm, arm, and out!—
If this which he avouches does appear,
There is nor flying hence nor tarrying here.
I 'gin to be aweary of the sun,
And wish th' estate o' th' world were now undone.—
Ring the alarum bell!—Blow, wind! come, wrack!
At least we'll die with harness on our back.

They exit the castle to enter the field of battle, accompanied by trumpeters.

ACT FIVE

SCENE SIX

In a field before Macbeth's castle, Malcolm, Siward, Macduff and their army enter camouflaged by branches, with drummers, and flags flying.

MODERN TRANSLATION:

ORIGINAL LANGUAGE:

(1-6) **MALCOLM.**
We're now near enough. Throw away the branches and show them who you really are.

They throw down the branches.

My worthy uncle Siward, you will lead the first battle with your son. Macduff and I will go wherever's needed, according to our battle plans.

(1-6) ***MALCOLM.***
Now near enough. Your leafy screens throw down,
And show like those you are.—You, worthy uncle,
Shall with my cousin, your right noble son,
Lead our first battle: worthy Macduff and we
Shall take upon's what else remains to do,
According to our order.

(6-8) **SIWARD.**
I wish you well. If we meet the tyrant's army tonight, then we must fight them. Restraint in this case would be the equivalent of a defeat.

(6-8) ***SIWARD.***
Fare you well.—
Do we but find the tyrant's power tonight,

Let us be beaten, if we cannot fight.

(9-10) **MACDUFF.**
Make our trumpets sing, blow hard with your breath,
These blaring messengers of blood and death.

(9-10) ***MACDUFF.***
Make all our trumpets speak; give them all breath,
Those clamorous harbingers of blood and death.

The army marches forth and enters into battle.

ACT FIVE

SCENE SEVEN

In another part of the field, Macbeth stands alone.

MODERN TRANSLATION:

(1-4) **MACBETH.**
They have me tied to a stake. I cannot escape. I'm like a baited bear waiting to be set upon by dogs. So like a bear I must fight on. Who was not of a woman born?

That's all I must fear. It is him or none that can defeat me.

Young Siward enters.

(5) **YOUNG SIWARD.**
What is your name?

(6) **MACBETH.**
You'd be frightened if you heard it.

ORIGINAL LANGUAGE:

(1-4) MACBETH.
They have tied me to a stake. I cannot fly,
But, bear-like I must fight the course.—What's he
That was not born of woman? Such a one
Am I to fear, or none.

Enter young Siward.

(5) ***YOUNG SIWARD.***
What is thy name?

(6) MACBETH.
Thou'lt be afraid to hear it.

(7-8) **YOUNG SIWARD.**
I'd not be afraid of any name you can claim, even if it was famed in the bowels of hell.

(7-8) YOUNG SIWARD.
No; though thou call'st thyself a hotter name
Than any is in hell.

(8) **MACBETH.**
I am Macbeth.

(8) MACBETH.
My name's Macbeth.

(9-10) **YOUNG SIWARD.**
The devil himself could not have pronounced a name more hateful to my ear.

(9-10) YOUNG SIWARD.
The devil himself could not pronounce a title
More hateful to mine ear.

(10) **MACBETH.**
Nor a name more terrifying.

(10) MACBETH.
No, nor more fearful.

(11-12) **YOUNG SIWARD.**
You lie, you abhorrent tyrant! Terrifying? I'll prove that's a lie with my sword.

Macbeth and Young Siward fight.
Young Siward is killed.

(11-12) YOUNG SIWARD.
Thou liest, abhorred tyrant. With my sword
I'll prove the lie thou speak'st.

They fight, and young Siward is slain.

(12-14) **MACBETH.**
Ha! You are of a woman born!

I smile at swords, and laugh with scorn,
If held by one of woman born.

(12-14) MACBETH.
Thou wast born of woman.
But swords I smile at, weapons laugh to scorn,
Brandish'd by man that's of a woman born.

Macbeth moves on, leaving Young Siward's corpse behind.

ACT FIVE

SCENE EIGHT

In another part of the field, Macduff walks determinedly.

MODERN TRANSLATION:

ORIGINAL LANGUAGE:

(1-10) **MACDUFF.**
The noise is coming from that way. Show your face, tyrant. If you are killed, but not by my sword, then my wife and children's ghosts will continue to haunt me. I don't wish to fight your miserable hired soldiers.

Either I fight you, Macbeth, or I won't spot my sword with any blood. The only blood it thirsts for is yours.

A trumpet plays.

It must be him – that trumpet's blast is to announce an important man.

Oh, Fortune, please let me find him. And if you do, I'll ask nothing more of you in this life.

(1-10) ***MACDUFF.***
That way the noise is.—Tyrant, show thy face!
If thou be'st slain and with no stroke of mine,
My wife and children's ghosts will haunt me still.
I cannot strike at wretched kerns, whose arms
Are hired to bear their staves. Either thou, Macbeth,
Or else my sword, with an unbatter'd edge,
I sheathe again undeeded. There thou shouldst be;
By this great clatter, one of greatest note

Seems bruited. Let me find him, Fortune!
And more I beg not.

Macduff scurries forth.

ACT FIVE

SCENE NINE

Malcolm and Siward walk together, approaching Macbeth's castle gates.

MODERN TRANSLATION:

ORIGINAL LANGUAGE:

(1-5) **SIWARD.**
This way, my lord. The castle's been surrendered peacefully. Most of the tyrant's men support our cause. And for those who don't, our noble lords are bravely playing their part. Your victory is almost ready to be announced. The fat lady is about to sing. There is not much more we can do.

(1-5) ***SIWARD.***
This way, my lord;—the castle's gently render'd:
The tyrant's people on both sides do fight;
The noble thanes do bravely in the war,
The day almost itself professes yours,
And little is to do.

(5-6) **MALCOLM.**
Yes, all our opponents fight as if they were on our side.

(5-6) ***MALCOLM.***
We have met with foes
That strike beside us.

(6) **SIWARD.**
Enter the castle, sir.

(6) ***SIWARD.***
Enter, sir, the castle.

Malcolm and Siward enter the castle together as conquerors.

ACT FIVE

SCENE TEN

Whilst in another part of the field, Macbeth waits alone.

MODERN TRANSLATION:

ORIGINAL LANGUAGE:

(1-3) **MACBETH.**
I'm not going to play the Roman fool and use my sword to kill myself. If I come across any that breathe, I'll kill them instead. The wounds will suit them much better.

Macduff enters behind Macbeth.

(1-3) ***MACBETH.***
Why should I play the Roman fool, and die
On mine own sword? whiles I see lives, the gashes
Do better upon them.

Enter Macduff.

(3) **MACDUFF.**
Turn around, you dog of hell, turn around!

(3) ***MACDUFF.***
Turn, hell-hound, turn!

(4-6) **MACBETH.**
Out of all the men I've killed, I've managed to avoid you. But stand back! The taste of your family's blood has already made me sick once.

(4-6) ***MACBETH.***
Of all men else I have avoided thee:
But get thee back; my soul is too much charg'd
With blood of thine already.

(6-8) **MACDUFF.**
I have no words.

Perhaps my sword can speak for me. You're such a repugnant villain that language cannot articulate your vileness.

They fight.

(6-8) ***MACDUFF.***
I have no words;
My voice is in my sword: thou bloodier villain
Than terms can give thee out!

They fight.

(8-13) **MACBETH.**
You're wasting your effort, friend. You have about as much chance of being able to wound the air, as you do of being able to wound me. Expend your effort on someone more vulnerable. I lead a charmed life. The witches told me I cannot be killed by one of woman born.

(8-13) ***MACBETH.***
Thou losest labour:
As easy mayst thou the intrenchant air
With thy keen sword impress, as make me bleed:
Let fall thy blade on vulnerable crests;
I bear a charmed life, which must not yield
To one of woman born.

(13-16) **MACDUFF.**
Ha! That charmed life is about to become one of despair, Macbeth. I'd love it if the evil spirits that you serve were the ones to tell you that I, Macduff, was wrenched from his mother's womb prematurely, by caesarean, so not technically of a woman born.

(13-16) ***MACDUFF.***
Despair thy charm;
And let the angel whom thou still hast serv'd
Tell thee, Macduff was from his mother's womb
Untimely ripp'd.

(17-22) **MACBETH.**
I curse the tongue that speaks these words! A caesarean!

My spirit is choking. Those vacillating witches. Those unreliable equivocators. I'm made the fool. My gullible senses hoodwinked by their tricky double-meanings. But my naïve ears only heard what my expectant hopes desired. I can fight no more.

Macbeth lets his shield fall to the ground.

(17-22) ***MACBETH.***
Accursed be that tongue that tells me so,
For it hath cow'd my better part of man!
And be these juggling fiends no more believ'd,
That palter with us in a double sense;
That keep the word of promise to our ear,
And break it to our hope!—I'll not fight with thee.

(23-27) **MACDUFF.**
Then surrender, coward. And become an exhibit of wickedness, on show like the other freaks of nature whom we cruelly make a spectacle.

Picture this, on a publicity poster, your face engraved with the slogan: 'Line up, line up, come see the world's most horrifying living creature: the terrible tyrant Macbeth'.

(23-27) ***MACDUFF.***
Then yield thee, coward,
And live to be the show and gaze o' th' time.
We'll have thee, as our rarer monsters are,
Painted upon a pole, and underwrit,
"Here may you see the tyrant."

(27-34) **MACBETH.**
No, I will not surrender and kiss the ground beneath that mere boy Malcolm's feet.

Macbeth picks his shield back up off the ground.

Nor will I succumb to the curses of those hags. Maybe Birnam Wood has come to Dunsinane Hill, and maybe you are not of woman born. But I will still fight to the end. My shield is ready.

Fight, Macduff! Do your best, I'll do my worst. Let he who submits first be damned and cursed.

(27-34) ***MACBETH.***
I will not yield,

To kiss the ground before young Malcolm's feet,
And to be baited with the rabble's curse.
Though Birnam wood be come to Dunsinane,
And thou oppos'd, being of no woman born,
Yet I will try the last. Before my body
I throw my warlike shield: lay on, Macduff;
And damn'd be him that first cries, "Hold, enough!"

Macbeth and Macduff fight, till Macbeth is killed. Macduff beheads Macbeth with his sword, and carries off his decapitated head.

ACT FIVE

SCENE ELEVEN

Before the castle gates, trumpets play to signify the end of the battle. Malcolm, Siward, Ross and many lords and soldiers gather joyfully, with trumpeters, drummers and flags flying.

MODERN TRANSLATION:

ORIGINAL LANGUAGE:

(1) **MALCOLM.**
I do wish our absent friends were here.

(1) MALCOLM.
I would the friends we miss were safe arriv'd.

(2-3) **SIWARD.**
Some must always die, but looking at this great crowd of soldiers here, it appears we have gained our victory at little cost.

(2-3) SIWARD.
Some must go off; and yet, by these I see,
So great a day as this is cheaply bought.

(4) **MALCOLM.**
Though Macduff is still missing, and your noble son, sir.

(4) MALCOLM.
Macduff is missing, and your noble son.

(5-9) **ROSS.**
Your son, my lord, has paid the price that a good soldier always owes. Perhaps only a short time has passed since he was but a child. But take comfort in the fact that the minute he became a man, he proved himself instantly as a brave warrior. And he died known to all as a fearless and worthy man, though you must still think of him as your boy.

(5-9) ***ROSS.***
Your son, my lord, has paid a soldier's debt:
He only liv'd but till he was a man;
The which no sooner had his prowess confirm'd
In the unshrinking station where he fought,
But like a man he died.

(9) **SIWARD.**
Is it true? Is he dead?

(9) ***SIWARD.***
Then he is dead?

(10-12) **ROSS.**
Yes, my lord, and he has been carried from the field of battle in which he died. Now, your sorrow cannot be measured by how brave and worthy he was, for if it was, your sorrow would never cease.

(10-12) ***ROSS.***
Ay, and brought off the field. Your cause of sorrow
Must not be measur'd by his worth, for then
It hath no end.

(12) **SIWARD.**
But he was wounded charging the enemy directly, not in the back as he retreated?

(12) ***SIWARD.***
Had he his hurts before?

(13) **ROSS.**
Yes, my lord, he was charging the enemy bravely.

(13) ***ROSS.***
Ay, on the front.

(13-16) **SIWARD.**
Well then, he died as a soldier should and in God's honour. Even if I had as many sons as I have hairs, I could not wish one of them a better way to die.

So, his bell's been tolled, his death knell's been rung,
And he, my sweet son, is now dead and done.

(13-16) ***SIWARD.***
Why then, God's soldier be he!
Had I as many sons as I have hairs,
I would not wish them to a fairer death:
And so his knell is knoll'd.

(16-17) **MALCOLM.**
But he is still worth more sorrow than that, and I will pay that debt for him.

(16-17) ***MALCOLM.***
He's worth more sorrow,
And that I'll spend for him.

(17-19) **SIWARD.**
No, he's worth no more. They say he died bravely and in my honour. 'God rest his soul' is all that needs be said. But, look, here comes our consolation.

Macduff enters, with Macbeth's decapitated head on a pole.

(17-19) ***SIWARD.***
He's worth no more.
They say he parted well and paid his score:
And so, God be with him!—Here comes newer comfort.

Enter Macduff with Macbeth's head.

(20-25) **MACDUFF.**
Hail the King! For that is your title now, King Malcolm!

And behold the tyrant's decapitated head upon this pole. We are now free from tyranny!

I see you are surrounded by all our nobles, those pearls of our kingdom, who I suspect must be hailing you in their minds' ears alone.

But I ask them all to join me boisterously and proclaim out loud: 'Hail, Malcolm, King of Scotland!'

(20-25) ***MACDUFF.***
Hail, King, for so thou art. Behold, where stands
Th' usurper's cursed head: the time is free.
I see thee compass'd with thy kingdom's pearl,
That speak my salutation in their minds;
Whose voices I desire aloud with mine,—
Hail, King of Scotland!

(15) **ALL EXCEPT MALCOLM.**
Hail, Malcolm, King of Scotland!

Trumpets play.

(15) ***ALL EXCEPT MALCOLM.***
Hail, King of Scotland!

Flourish.

(26-41) **MALCOLM.**
It will not be long before I can reward you all, with more than my just my everlasting love, for your loyalty, and service to me. Though I'll always remain forever in your debts. But for now, my lords and kin, I pronounce you all earls, the first ever to be honoured with this title in all of Scotland's history.

The other actions I need to take in this new era, such as calling home our exiled friends overseas, who fled the snares of my predecessors' tyranny. And putting on trial the brutal representatives of that dead butcher and his vile queen, who, by the way, as we suspected, used her violent hands to take her own life. These undertakings, and whatever else needs to be done, we will perform, God willing, to the appropriate degree, at the appropriate time, and in the appropriate place.

But to conclude, thanks to all who's around,
And let's head off to Scone, to see me crowned.

(26-41) ***MALCOLM.***
We shall not spend a large expense of time
Before we reckon with your several loves,
And make us even with you. My thanes and kinsmen,
Henceforth be earls, the first that ever Scotland
In such an honour nam'd. What's more to do,
Which would be planted newly with the time,—
As calling home our exil'd friends abroad,
That fled the snares of watchful tyranny;
Producing forth the cruel ministers
Of this dead butcher, and his fiend-like queen,
Who, as 'tis thought, by self and violent hands
Took off her life;—this, and what needful else
That calls upon us, by the grace of Grace,
We will perform in measure, time, and place.
So thanks to all at once, and to each one,
Whom we invite to see us crown'd at Scone.

The flags wave and trumpets play. They all depart, joining Malcolm on the road to Scone, where he will be crowned King of Scotland!

THE END

Printed in Great Britain
by Amazon